Anthony Gilbert and The Murder Room

››› This title is part of The Murder Room, our series dedicated to making available out-of-print or hard-to-find titles by classic crime writers.

Crime fiction has always held up a mirror to society. The Victorians were fascinated by sensational murder and the emerging science of detection; now we are obsessed with the forensic detail of violent death. And no other genre has so captivated and enthralled readers.

Vast troves of classic crime writing have for a long time been unavailable to all but the most dedicated frequenters of second-hand bookshops. The advent of digital publishing means that we are now able to bring you the backlists of a huge range of titles by classic and contemporary crime writers, some of which have been out of print for decades.

From the genteel amateur private eyes of the Golden Age and the femmes fatales of pulp fiction, to the morally ambiguous hard-boiled detectives of mid twentieth-century America and their descendants who walk our twenty-first century streets, The Murder Room has it all. ›››

The Murder Room
Where Criminal Minds Meet

themurderroom.com

Anthony Gilbert (1899–1973)

Anthony Gilbert was the pen name of Lucy Beatrice Malleson. Born in London, she spent all her life there, and her affection for the city is clear from the strong sense of character and place in evidence in her work. She published 69 crime novels, 51 of which featured her best known character, Arthur Crook, a vulgar London lawyer totally (and deliberately) unlike the aristocratic detectives, such as Lord Peter Wimsey, who dominated the mystery field at the time. She also wrote more than 25 radio plays, which were broadcast in Great Britain and overseas. Her thriller *The Woman in Red* (1941) was broadcast in the United States by CBS and made into a film in 1945 under the title *My Name is Julia Ross*. She was an early member of the British Detection Club, which, along with Dorothy L. Sayers, she prevented from disintegrating during World War II. Malleson published her autobiography, *Three-a-Penny*, in 1940, and wrote numerous short stories, which were published in several anthologies and in such periodicals as *Ellery Queen's Mystery Magazine* and *The Saint*. The short story 'You Can't Hang Twice' received a Queens award in 1946. She never married, and evidence of her feminism is elegantly expressed in much of her work.

By Anthony Gilbert

Scott Egerton series

Tragedy at Freyne (1927)
The Murder of Mrs Davenport (1928)
Death at Four Corners (1929)
The Mystery of the Open Window (1929)
The Night of the Fog (1930)
The Body on the Beam (1932)
The Long Shadow (1932)
The Musical Comedy Crime (1933)
An Old Lady Dies (1934)
The Man Who Was Too Clever (1935)

Mr Crook Murder Mystery series

Murder by Experts (1936)
The Man Who Wasn't There (1937)
Murder Has No Tongue (1937)
Treason in My Breast (1938)
The Bell of Death (1939)
Dear Dead Woman (1940)
aka *Death Takes a Redhead*
The Vanishing Corpse (1941)
aka *She Vanished in the Dawn*
The Woman in Red (1941)
aka *The Mystery of the Woman in Red*
Death in the Blackout (1942)
aka *The Case of the Tea-Cosy's Aunt*
Something Nasty in the Woodshed (1942)
aka *Mystery in the Woodshed*
The Mouse Who Wouldn't Play Ball (1943)
aka *30 Days to Live*
He Came by Night (1944)
aka *Death at the Door*
The Scarlet Button (1944)
aka *Murder Is Cheap*
A Spy for Mr Crook (1944)
The Black Stage (1945)
aka *Murder Cheats the Bride*
Don't Open the Door (1945)
aka *Death Lifts the Latch*
Lift Up the Lid (1945)
aka *The Innocent Bottle*
The Spinster's Secret (1946)
aka *By Hook or by Crook*
Death in the Wrong Room (1947)
Die in the Dark (1947)
aka *The Missing Widow*
Death Knocks Three Times (1949)
Murder Comes Home (1950)
A Nice Cup of Tea (1950)
aka *The Wrong Body*

Lady-Killer (1951)
Miss Pinnegar Disappears (1952)
aka *A Case for Mr Crook*
Footsteps Behind Me (1953)
aka *Black Death*
Snake in the Grass (1954)
aka *Death Won't Wait*
Is She Dead Too? (1955)
aka *A Question of Murder*
And Death Came Too (1956)
Riddle of a Lady (1956)
Give Death a Name (1957)
Death Against the Clock (1958)
Death Takes a Wife (1959)
aka *Death Casts a Long Shadow*
Third Crime Lucky (1959)
aka *Prelude to Murder*
Out for the Kill (1960)
She Shall Die (1961)
aka *After the Verdict*
Uncertain Death (1961)
No Dust in the Attic (1962)
Ring for a Noose (1963)
The Fingerprint (1964)
The Voice (1964)
aka *Knock, Knock! Who's There?*
Passenger to Nowhere (1965)
The Looking Glass Murder (1966)
The Visitor (1967)
Night Encounter (1968)
aka *Murder Anonymous*
Missing from Her Home (1969)
Death Wears a Mask (1970)
aka *Mr Crook Lifts the Mask*
Murder is a Waiting Game (1972)
Tenant for the Tomb (1971)
A Nice Little Killing (1974)

Standalone Novels

The Case Against Andrew Fane (1931)
Death in Fancy Dress (1933)
The Man in Button Boots (1934)
Courtier to Death (1936)
aka *The Dover Train Mystery*
The Clock in the Hatbox (1939)

Ring for a Noose

Anthony Gilbert

An Orion book

This edition published by
The Orion Publishing Group Ltd
Orion House
5 Upper St Martin's Lane
London WC2H 9EA

An Hachette UK company
A CIP catalogue record for this book is available from the British Library

ISBN 978 1 4719 1022 7

www.orionbooks.co.uk

CHAPTER I

On a demn'd moist unpleasant evening in early spring Mr. Arthur Crook lifted his receiver and found his telephone was out of order.

"Another unofficial strike," he deplored, reaching for his appalling brown bowler hat.

It was nine o'clock and many men might have decided to call it a day, but Crook was one of those to whom darkness and light are both alike, and he decided to put in a call from the telephone booth in Brandon Passage. This passage was a long narrow path running behind his house, and joining the normally busy main street with a secondary highway near Palace Stadium.

Mr. Crook's client was a man of fearful heart, who might pass out before morning if he wasn't reassured, so out Crook went right into the heart of a mystery. The passage was nearly as dark as Tennyson's famous black bat. The fog, that had been the colour of weak gravy when Crook returned from Bloomsbury Street, was turning into a pea-souper. The economical lights at either end of the street passage were crowned with a faint yellowish aureole, but a spot of illumination was added by a lamp left near the foot of the kiosk by builders who were repairing the wall of a small plastics factory that backed on the passage.

The world into which he marched seemed as quiet as a grave; only in the main street the infrequent traffic bumbled along like an army of the blind; and suddenly Crook's skin began to tingle as if once again he hovered on the verge of something dangerous—and irresistible. The small red lamp that to the imaginative might have suggested blood was to him the star of hope.

Having assured his client that cowards die many times but brave men only once and not on that occasion, with Arthur Crook to frank you, in the little covered shed, he moved towards the High Street. Such traffic as was still unwise enough to be abroad crept along as if going to the funeral of the sun, and not many mourners at that. Normally Crook repaired to The Two Chairmen which served him as a club, but in view of the weather, and the fact that it seemed momentarily deteriorating, he turned for once into the nearer Duck and Daisy. This was new ground to him, he hadn't been inside the place since the advent of the new licensee more than two years earlier. Under the old man it had had a bad name, by which he meant the beer hadn't been up to standard, though it was a Free House and the licensee could buy where he pleased. His first sight of the public bar was anything but reassuring. A few chaps, who could have walked on in a Hitchcock thriller as funeral mutes, were standing about looking as if they were doing their weekly penance. The landlord, whose name was Prentiss and who called Crook sir, looked as if he were in the right place for the company. Crook even considered backing out and making for The Chairmen but that warning tingle kept him where he was. No cat-loving, fortune-telling spinster backed her hunches more enthusiastically than Arthur Crook.

"Quiet to-night," he offered, buying his usual pint and disposing of it in his usual manner, open the uvula and let it flow down in one stupendous swallow. He pushed the tankard across for a refill.

"It's no night to be out," returned Prentiss, and his voice matched his appearance—like a passing bell, thought Crook. Dong. Dong. Dong. "Still it'll fill up later. There's a meeting at St. Katharine's Hall to-night."

Crook knew the place, a big bleak erection put up at the turn of the century and apparently much in demand for jumble sales and what were called flannel dances. But he couldn't imagine who was going to turn out for any kind of meeting in this weather when they could stay nice and cosy round the goggle-box.

"You'd be surprised," said Prentiss, reading his thought. "Mind you, they've got Lady Connie there to-night."

"Have they, by gum?" Crook brightened. No theatregoer and not much of a TV viewer, he nevertheless knew the name at once. "If she's a patch on her grannie she's worth coming through a blitz to see. I remember," he went on, thoughtfully turning the tankard in his hands, "Vera Golightly—the names they chose—back in '18, giving a show to the troops. She must have been forty plus then but most of our lot thought they'd been blown up in their sleep and awakened in heaven."

She had been, he remembered, the most glamorous show-girl of her age, an age when stage-door Johnnies queued up for hours to drink champagne out of tiny satin slippers and the Queens of the Chorus wore cartwheel hats costing sixty sovereigns apiece. He heaved a gusty sigh for the dear dead days, etc.

"Don't you ever see her on the television?" Prentiss asked and Crook said he didn't have much time. He noted with approval there was no TV set here, but the landlord spoilt that by saying he'd got one in the Private. Two or three chaps turned up regularly, they'd be along to-night any minute now, home from home it was to them and one of these days they'd probably ask him to put up beds for them. In which case, thought the unregenerate Mr. Crook, they wouldn't notice any appreciable difference when they were shovelled into the grave.

"What's Lady C. on about this evening? A sort of private quiz?"

Because that was her lay. Sensibly realising that the day of the show-girl is over and that boatloads of youngsters, brighter mentally and just as good-looking, were available for the asking, she'd taken her big chance and married Lord Charles Hunter at the beginning of the war. Now she was in perpetual demand by both channels for panel games and did a little discreet advertising, and that enabled Lord Charles to lose comfortably at cards while she raked the shekels in. It was an arrangement that appeared to suit them both admirably. They were quoted everywhere when people had to list the ten happiest married couples in the public eye.

"She's speaking for the Peace Brigade," said Prentiss,

still about as lively as a tombstone. " You may have heard of them, one of those associations that stump the country. . . ."

" Ban the Bomb. Down with Defences. I know. Who finances 'em ? "

" They take up collections and they run a monthly paper they print themselves, and they do house-to-house visiting."

Crook's eyes widened. " Well, that's as good a way as any of getting to know the lie of the land," he admitted. It was second nature to him to look for criminal intent behind the most modest enterprise. " This Lady C. now —what does she know about refugees ? "

" Well, it's the name really." Prentiss—his regulars, who weren't many, called him Jim—drew a couple of pints for a chap who looked as if it wouldn't surprise him to find a few tadpoles thrown in. Coins chinked on the counter. " And she is a draw," he went on, coming back. " They've got a real refugee talking, came out of Hungary at the time of the revolution. Not that they're much good for trade," he added, the faint note of enthusiasm dying out of his voice. " They come along here in case they can pick up a few converts, chaps who've been at the meeting, and have a pint apiece, and then they go off to the Casbah to do their real drinking—that's a coffee house in Morley Street, in case you didn't know."

Crook didn't, and why on earth should he, he wondered ? He made his own coffee in a saucepan, strong as Samson and black as night, and no nonsense about sugar and cream.

" My sister's girl goes along with the Brigade," Prentiss volunteered. There was none of that hearty bonhomie here that you found at the Chairmen. " My sister gets a bit worried, she should be thinking about getting a husband, she says, but what I say is they make a nice change from the Never-Had-It-So-Good brigade. They don't like the way the world's shaping and I don't blame 'em. But then the young take life a lot more seriously than we did, wouldn't you say ? "

" I don't know about you," retorted Crook. " But when

I was seventeen I was jumping in and out of shell holes in France, trying to dodge the Jerries, and I wasn't particularly approving of the world either. Only in those days there was less nattering. Poor bloody Tommy just got on with it and nobody paid to hear him orate from a platform, not even in a church hall. Hallo, is this your lot ?"

The door was hurled open and a stream of young people—later he found there were only five of them but at the time they seemed like an army—flowed in. The atmosphere brightened instantly and so did Mr. Crook. At their head was a remarkably good-looking young man (make an A.1 con. man if he's got brains to match his looks, was Crook's typical reflection) followed by a sturdy dark girl wearing the jeans that Crook, in his old-fashioned way, deplored. The only other girl in the party, he saw with relief, was dressed like a female, but whatever she'd been wearing she'd have attracted attention. Much taller than her companion, she had a very fair skin and long beautiful hands. She walked quite beautifully, too. Later, when he learned she was on the stage (though not far on it, she confessed frankly) he wasn't at all surprised. A couple of youths followed, all wearing what seemed to be the uniform for their type, high-necked sweaters and raincoats (or duffel coats and not a penny to choose between them), shoes that were a shade too pointed for his taste, and they all carried brief-cases like a lot of seedy F.O. officials.

" No Lady Connie ? " mourned Mr. Crook aloud.

They stared as though a bit of the furniture had spoken. Then the dark girl, whose name turned out to be Ruth, said, " You'll have to go to the Savoy if you want to see her. You should have been at the meeting. . . ."

" Working for the meat that perisheth," explained Mr. Crook, hurriedly.

" Anyway, who wants to go to the Savoy ? " continued Ruth, scornfully.

The pretty girl (Juliet Ware—he'd sorted out all their names by the end of the evening) opened her wide blue eyes and said, " I was hoping she'd ask us all." She looked round. " Did Torquil go ? "

" I don't think he was invited. Only Paul. And that was because she had another Hungarian refugee meeting her there."

" Why wasn't he at the meeting ? " demanded Ruth. You could see the type she was, she'd never miss a trick.

" Perhaps he was working for the meat that perisheth," suggested the tall handsome young man who had led the procession. " Still, Paul didn't go. He's on to something on his own account."

" If he's not precious careful he'll be on to trouble on Torquil's account," said one of the other young men. " Oh, I dare say he's only trying to pull another refugee chestnut out of the fire, but Torquil's the boss, he oughtn't to be playing a lone hand."

" I wonder if there's such a thing as a refugee mentality," reflected Juliet, taking her modest half-pint from Rupert Bowen. " Thanks, Ru. I mean, I feel Paul would sooner leave a house by the fire-escape than walk through the door, even if it was open."

A thin brown chap whose mother had misguidedly called him Evelyn said something about a security complex. " You have to remember what he's been through. He lay up in the long grass on the wrong side of the wire. . . ."

" Oh no, Eve," breathed Rupert. " We could all tell that story in our sleep. One of these days the audience is going to get up and join in the chorus. I'm not knocking Paul and I dare say it all happened just the way he tells it, but it is—let's face it—a bit like listening to a gramophone record when the needle's stuck. It's about time old Tork sent him north to one of the other branches."

" Who's going to do the house-to-house visiting if he goes north ? " Ruth inquired. " You know the rest of us haven't the time, and no one can deny he's good at it. If Torquil had approached Lady Connie all he'd have got would have been a nice letter explaining why it was out of the question."

" A lot he'd have cared. She's nothing but a glorified chorus girl to him. He'd prefer a skeleton from one of the camps on the platform."

" Yes, well, I dare say that would have its attractions, too," agreed Colin Grant, the fifth member of the party.

Jim leaned across the bar. " This gentleman remembers Lady Connie's grandmother," he said.

" The Vera Lynn of our day," Crook amplified.

He couldn't even be certain if the allusion went home. A generation can be as wide as the gap that separates life from death. " Talk about heavenly visions," he added.

They didn't even pretend to be interested. Full marks for single-mindedness, minus one for manners, he thought.

" It's too bad about Jos," continued Colin. (Jos ? Male ? Female ? Crook gave up.) " The one night we have a really full house he has to be in the Midlands arranging the Refugee Exhibition. I thought he was going to catch the earlier train."

" There's a fog to-night or had it escaped your notice ? " They might all buy their drink in half-pint mugs, but in their own estimation the place belonged to them.

Then the door opened again with some violence and a tall dark chap came in, and all the winds of Heaven seemed to follow him. Crook found himself suddenly sitting bolt upright, for here, unless he was much mistaken, was the reason for that anticipatory thrill he'd experienced in the passage. Trouble was his business and here was a man who would be followed by every kind of trouble, as Don Quixote had been followed by his faithful Sancho. Not a town type, the sort you'd expect to find working on the land, in the Outer Hebrides, say, reflected Crook, who'd never been there. He wore the inevitable turtle-necked sweater and the sort of trousers a dustman wouldn't give you a thank you for, and carried a raincoat over his arm. He came storming across to the group and Rupert politely got up and bought him a pint. " Expecting a stormy passage," decided Crook.

" Good meeting, didn't you think ? " suggested Colin quickly. " Good kitty anyway."

Torquil Holland took the tankard from his lieutenant's hand almost as if he didn't know what he was doing. His dark eyes under their thick brows were as hard as coals.

"Where's Paul?"

"He's said he'd be seeing us in the Casbah later on."

"And meantime, I suppose, he's drinking champagne in the Savoy. I understand she drinks nothing else."

"As a matter of fact, Tork, he isn't. He's got some contact he was meeting, he'll tell you about it later. Come to that, I think Lady C. was a bit disappointed. I suppose she thought the two refugees could play each other off."

Ruth, who was watching Torquil's face, said, "She had a refugee over from the States on a business trip—something to do with Lord Charles really, but I gather he turns all the social side over to her."

"And she told Paul and Paul wouldn't go?"

"If he was meeting this other chap . . ."

"What other chap?"

"Well, I don't know. I did get the idea he might be trying to smuggle someone in from the other side of the Berlin wall."

"What's all this about smuggling? If he can get out, this country isn't going to refuse him an entrance visa."

"I think it's a bit more complicated than that," murmured Evelyn. "Trouble over a frontier guard or something."

"You'd be a gift to conjurors, all that faith going begging," Torquil told him; he sounded as disagreeable as a bear deprived of its honey ration. "Like to have a small bet?"

He slammed down his tankard and Crook unobtrusively signed to Jim to fill it up again. This chap—he felt it in his bones—was going to be worth a lot more to him than the price of a pint of wallop.

"Old Tork's off on another of his McCarthy campaigns," groaned Colin.

"O.K.," said Torquil, taking the now-filled tankard without apparently noticing it had ever been empty. "Tell me this—how long have we known Paul Luzky?"

"Well, it's a bit over two years, isn't it, Jim?"

"Something like that," the landlord agreed.

"And how much do we know about him? Have we ever met anyone who recognised him as coming from Hungary?

Does he ever get letters from home, or vary his speech in the least to include later developments since the Revolution? Why, has anyone here even seen a photograph of any of his people—his wife, his parents—we know they were left behind. . . .?"

"He told me his wife had been killed," murmured Juliet.

"Anyway, when you're flying for your life you don't stop to collect the family photograph album."

"That's just what you do do," contradicted Torquil. "It's the instinct of every refugee. He's never made the smallest effort to try and get the old people over. . . ."

"Probably they don't want to come. Tork, what is all this in aid of? I vetted him when he first turned up here in answer to Jim's advertisement. He had all his papers, passport, identification—we were beginning to find it hard to get new speakers and he was a bit of a misfit behind the bar—we checked with the Aliens Office, they had his record, he'd notified them of his most recent change of address—what are you trying to say?"

"That I don't believe he's ever been nearer Hungary than the Isle of Wight."

The clamour rose at once. "He's got papers," Rupert insisted.

"I could knock you out and pinch your passport, but that wouldn't make me Rupert Bowen."

"He speaks fluent German. . . ."

"So do I, and I was born in Cambridge."

It was Ruth the Fearless who said in her downright fashion, "Then, Torquil, you mean you think . . ."

"I think he's a crook. I've had my doubts about him for some time, but I couldn't take any action without something in the nature of proof. It didn't seem to me natural that he should apparently know London twenty times as well as he knows Budapest, where, according to himself, he spent the first twenty-five years of his life. I don't understand why a Hungarian refugee appears to be completely out of touch with all the other refugees who came over at the same time. Oh, I know a good many didn't remain, they went on to the States or Australia or New Zealand, if they could get in, but there must be one or two—he doesn't even get cards at Christmas, he's got no links whatsoever. Even when he's billed to speak none of them turn up to shake him by the hand. Oh, he says they've become integrated, they're British citizens many of them or are in for British citizenship, they don't want to remember the past, but it's all too vague to be true. Have any of you ever heard him make one definite statement he couldn't have got out of a newspaper? It's always a man I used to know, a family I was familiar with, but try and pin him down and he floats off like an air balloon. And why? Don't tell me it's because he doesn't want to remember the past. That's how he makes his living, recalling the past. And that's another thing. He never looks particularly shabby, you never see him waiting in the bus queue on a wet evening, but according to him he came over here with absolutely nothing, he answered Jim's advertisement because he was out of a job, though he'd never served in a bar before—what was he in his own country?"

"He worked in a factory, tool-making; and he made a bit on the side waiting in the evening. It's quite usual out there, according to him. You become a relief waiter and the chap you're relieving goes off and plays in a band. He still does that, you know, waits at banquets as a spare in his free time. That's probably the answer to your question as to how he gets a living."

"Well, I know what we pay him for looking after the office, and we don't pretend it's a living wage. I told him from the start only to regard it as temporary and as soon as he heard of something better to go ahead. And he doesn't even try. He could get a good wage in a machine shop."

Evelyn said something about the unions. "I don't believe they'd bar him," said Torquil, "not if he's the genuine article. But in any case there are non-union shops. And then to-night he's asked to drink champagne at the Savoy—and I never knew such a social hound—to meet another refugee and he oils off—Why? I'll tell you. He knows he can't hold his own against the genuine article.

Besides, there's always the chance this other fellow will be curious about the real Paul Luzky."

" Not curious enough to come to the meeting," said Rupert, smartly. " It's just as probable there's some sort of feud—he's a sullen type, you know, though he can turn on the charm when he thinks it'll pay—he could have his own reasons for not wanting to meet him."

" Well, he'll be able to tell me to-night what those reasons are."

" Hold your horses, Tork," Rupert besought him. " Suppose, for the sake of argument, you're right, the chap is a phony, you don't want to go spreading the story far and wide. We shall look a proper lot of Charlies if it comes out that we've been stumping the country with a chap from Palmers Green or what-have-you."

" Rupert's right," Ruth agreed. They seemed to have forgotten Mr. Crook, and the other drinkers paid them not the slightest attention. Anyway they were clenched together in a sort of knot, cut off from the rest. Even Jim didn't seem to pay them much attention. Every now and again he disappeared into the Private Bar—he appeared to be running the place on his own to-night—and Crook leaned against the counter and wondered just where he himself came in. That he came in somewhere he didn't doubt for an instant.

" What's your suggestion then ? " asked Torquil. " That we just keep our big silly mouths shut and let this charlatan go on getting money by false pretences ? Because that's what it amounts to. Did no one ever tell you that men 'ull forgive you for forging their names to a cheque or even for running off with their wives, but they never, never forgive you for making them look fools?"

" We don't know for certain," protested Colin, and Torquil said, " I do. I suppose it's difficult to be on guard twenty-four hours a day. Mind you, I'd begun to have doubts some time ago, but I had to get some proof that they were justified. The night before last I was meeting a man in a pub, which was pretty crowded, and I caught sight of Paul talking to some stranger across the room. I wanted a word with him so I began to edge closer. Then I realised he was talking without a trace of accent to a man who called him Jack. He didn't see me, and I moved away again. I didn't want to start a scene there, but that's another point Master Paul's got to clear up when we meet."

"He's been over here for nearly six years," Colin protested. "He speaks pretty good English."

"He also speaks idiomatic English, which is unusual in a man who never saw this country, according to his own story, till he was twenty-five. And, however good his phraseology might become, it's not likely he'd ever lose a trace of his foreign accent. That's one of the reasons why I say he never saw Hungary in his life."

"Then how does he know so much about what happened?" Colin persisted. "He didn't get all that out of the press."

"Oh, I dare say he knew the real Paul Luzky, in fact, he has to, otherwise how would he know such a chap ever existed. He must have known him quite well, because a lot of his detail is undoubtedly authentic. But that doesn't make him a Hungarian. Are you going to tell me none of you ever had any doubts?"

There was a moment's silence. Then Rupert said, "O.K. I'll admit I was a bit foxed sometimes, details didn't altogether add up, but he'd been away a long time and memory can be treacherous, and in any case the last thing we want is a scandal. Face the facts, Torquil, we can't afford one."

"If what I suspect is true we've got one on our hands in any case," his leader retorted. But Rupert was persistent. "Not unless you insist. Say you tackle Paul and he admits it—what's the sense in spreading the story far and wide? You'll simply throw away five years' hard work. I don't know a lot about law but it might even result in a criminal prosecution, and the Brigade will be finished. I dare say we're only small beer, but you can't conceivably want that to happen."

Torquil was suddenly very quiet and courteous. "So we keep our mouths shut?"

"Don't you agree? After all, take the academic view. What has Paul done? He's got up on various platforms and told audiences what life was like, probably still is like, in Curtain countries. There's no reason to suppose his picture isn't the true one. You admit yourself he must have got his facts from an authentic source. We've used him to arouse sympathy and help rake in the shekels, he's done both. Can't you regard him like the actor who plays Henry VIII at the Old Vic ? Everyone knows he's not Henry VIII. . . ."

" Precisely. Everyone knows. I suppose it isn't possible," he added, slowly, " you had more than a suspicion that Paul was a phony ? "

Rupert started to get to his feet ; Colin caught his arm ; Crook regretfully upset a newly replenished tankard. And it was good beer, too. Some of it splashed on Juliet's dress and Crook was full of apologies.

" It doesn't matter," urged Juliet, and he saw that it didn't. Nothing mattered, so far as he could tell, but Torquil, and Torquil's reactions to the situation. But the diversion served its purpose.

" O.K.," Torquil said. " I take that back, though if you had suspicions I consider you should have mentioned them."

" You're such a sudden chap," Rupert grumbled. " Once you're on the warpath heads begin to roll. And I'd no proof, not even as much as you. In any case, it was becoming obvious we could not use Paul as a speaker much longer, we were agreeing that before you came in. Surely the best things now is to shunt him quietly . . ."

Crook looked at him with pity. Chap must be all of twenty-five and hardly knew he was born. A man who could put over an imposture like that for more than two years wasn't going to make any quiet exit. It was Ruth who put the question that was fascinating him.

" But why, Torquil ? " she insisted. " I mean, what was in it for Paul ? You've just said he could do a lot better for himself, so why this elaborate faking ? "

" That's something else he'll be able to explain," Torquil assured her, " when I see him at the Casbah."

" He won't be there yet," Juliet told him. " I don't know where he was seeing this man. . . ."

" I've got all night," said Torquil, swinging his raincoat over his shoulder.

The pacific Evelyn murmured that Paul might have answers to all these points, had Torquil considered that ?

" Oh, I'm sure he will," their leader agreed. " For his own sake, let's hope they're good ones."

On this dramatic line he swung out of the Duck and Daisy.

" Curtain on Act One," reflected Mr. Crook. " And by rights it should rise on a corpse."

The wind made by his departure had scarcely died away when Juliet rose.

" I'm going round to the Casbah," she announced.

" No wonder men were afraid of the Amazons," said Rupert, simply. " That's the one place I propose to avoid." He turned to the two other young men. " How about me and Col coming round to your place, Eve, and trying out those new records? If ever I saw murder in a man's face I saw it in Tork's to-night. Paul won't have to worry about his future if that's anything to go on. He won't need anything but a coffin by the time they're through."

And Crook, who always came up with the appropriate cliché, thought, " Many a true word spoken in jest," and recalled once again the premonition he had had as he battered his way into the passage a bare hour before.

" What's the idea, Julie ? " Evelyn asked, not replying to Rupert's question.

" I want to get there before Torquil and warn Paul. Unless one of you would like to take on the job," she added.

" We're cowards to a man," said Rupert, promptly. " Anyway, whose side are you on ? "

" Torquil's, of course. Need you ask ? I just don't think it's a good idea they should meet to-night, and if Paul isn't at the Casbah when Torquil arrives there'll be a time lag. . . ."

" And in the morning everything will be different. Is that the idea ? It won't, you know."

" Of course it won't. But it'll look different. Things always do. Torquil will have a chance to get things into perspective. Paul isn't worth wrecking things for."

She picked up her blue nylon mac and went out.

" All this going off the deep end," Rupert deplored, " only results in hitting your head on the bottom. And, so far as Tork is concerned, that 'ud be a pity, because he really does have some pretty sound ideas."

" So naturally," capped Ruth, "he doesn't take to it kindly when they're wrecked. I only hope Paul has sufficient sense to listen to Julie, if she gets there first, that is."

" Fancy old Paul being Jekyll and Hyde," Rupert mused. " All the same, Ruthie, you've got a point. Why hitch on to us ?"

" I'll give you three guesses," said Crook, unexpectedly. He put his big hand into his breast-pocket. " Just an emergency ration," he offered and dealt out some of his unconventional professional cards with the skill of a practised bridge player. " And it means what it says there," he went on. " All round the clock service. Don't look so startled. It wouldn't surprise me a bit if your chum found himself needing legal aid before all this blows over."

He supposed that to them he seemed a relic from the Ice Age. At all events his name didn't seem to ring any bells, but that only meant they hadn't been in his kind of trouble to date.

" No harm having an extra ace up your sleeve," conceded Rupert gracefully. And then Ruth said, " Let's have one more for the road and call it a day. I think," she added, " I'll calm my troubled mind with half an hour of Mr. Magoo. He's on at my local flea-pit and after to-night's session he'll be a positive rest-cure."

Adding, " This is on me " in a tone so determined that Crook, who had intended to do the honours, prudently withdrew, she moved to the bar. Crook thought, " Now if she was Torquil's man I could tuck up cosy in bed." He knew her type or believed he did. She had one of those neat little cat's faces that look soft and pliable, but are really as tough as rubber. And if she wore jeans, which he deplored, at least she didn't aggravate the offence by matching them with stiletto heels. Instead she wore sensible square-toed shoes (and polished them, which was another point in her favour), in which she could have started on a Ban the Bomb Campaign march as soon as the Casbah closed down. She came back after a minute with four glasses on a tray.

"I've had a word with Jim," she said. "I told him if Paul should turn up here to warn him to steer clear of the Casbah to-night. I know he told Julie he'd be going straight there but people do change their minds, don't they?"

She drank her half-pint standing, tied a red and black silk scarf round her head, pulled on a bright red plastic mac and collected a long slender brolly that she had leaned against the wall.

"What was the idea of bringing that?" Rupert asked. "It doesn't generally rain during a fog."

"Oh, I always take it to meetings," Ruth assured him. "Then I can give a good poke to anyone in the audience who's talking too much. There was a couple next to me this evening—I think I laddered her stocking." She looked affectionately at the ferrule of the red umbrella. "We're on first watch at the office to-morrow, aren't we, Ru? One of us better try and get in touch with Paul first thing and find out how the land lies."

Outside an ambulance went by with a shrill ringing of bells. "If there was any justice," Ruth continued calmly, "that would be for Paul, only life doesn't work that way. The man who said he'd never seen the righteous begging their bread ought to apply for a pair of National Health spectacles."

Another nice exit line, thought Crook. It had been an instructive evening, but so far as he was concerned it was over. At least, that's what he thought at the time. He looked round for a final one for the road, but Jim was off again in the Private, where for the first time he could hear the TV programme in full blast. Fancy straining your eyes watching mayhem on the goggle-box when you could have the real thing for the price of a few pints, he reflected.

But there was one point they all seemed to have missed, in its own way the most fascinating part of the affair.

If Torquil Holland was right and their precious Paul was an impostor, what had happened to the real article? And again he thought, "Three guesses, and I could give you back two with parsley round the dish."

: : : :

"This Paul character?" he asked Jim Prentiss when all the Peace Brigade had departed. "Does he do all his drinking at the Savoy?"

"Oh, is that where he is to-night? No, he comes along with the rest quite often. Not that they stop long. I hope there's not going to be trouble, not on my premises anyway," he added. "That girl left a message for him, if he should turn up. I don't like it," he added in worried tones.

"No skin off your nose," Crook consoled him, but Jim said, unsmiling as ever, "Well, but it was me introduced them. I'd advertised for someone to help behind the bar and he was one of the applicants, and, seeing he was a foreigner and said it wasn't too easy getting a job, I gave him a trial."

"And it didn't work out?" suggested the intelligent Mr. Crook. "So you palmed him on to your friends?"

"Well, there's no getting away from the fact that customers do like to see a woman on the premises," conceded Jim. "And somehow he didn't seem to catch on, though he was willing, I grant you that, very willing. Then one night he got talking to Mr. Bowen and it came out about his coming from Hungary and—Mr. Holland was on one of his trips getting facts, he's a great chap for getting about—anyway that's how it started, and in no time he was working for them, and I understood it was satisfactory all round. And I got a very good girl, Sally—she's not here to-night, got a touch of 'flu—but she knows how to tackle the gentlemen in the Private and she's smart as a whip, can attend to both bars in an emergency. And the customers like her. She's a widow," he added. "It's a wonder to me she hasn't got herself another husband. I'm a bachelor myself," he went on in the same tone that had made Crook think of the passing bell.

"You want to watch out," Crook advised him in friendly tones. "This Paul—he a lady's man?"

"He never said much. Consumed his own smoke, as they say. But good on the platform, I'll give him that. I went along to hear him once. Mind you, it wasn't treating me right if he didn't come from Hungary. It's not surprising that Mr. Holland's annoyed."

Crook goggled at the placid tone. Chap like this, he was thinking, you could let off a moon rocket in his back garden, and he'd only think it was a new sort of firework.

"You mark my words," he said heartily. "Something 'ull come of this. Let's hope it won't be human gore."

CHAPTER II

AT THE SAVOY, too, the conversation centred round Paul Luzky.

Lady Connie might be a bird-brain, as her husband sometimes averred, but she had a gift for happiness that was far to seek in these troublous times. People are hard-working, ambitious, far-sighted, but keeping up with the Joneses is a full-time occupation and leaves little space for the simpler virtues. To put it plainly, wherever Lady Connie appeared she seemed to bring the sun with her. On this particular evening, however, she felt as though a cloud had crossed her sky; she had been genuinely moved by what she had heard on the platform of St. Katharine's Hall, and though, of course, Hungary was a long time ago, the problem *per se* was as acute as ever. She couldn't pretend to regret Paul's inability to join her party, and she even wished she wasn't going to encounter another member of that disturbed race that evening. But when she saw her guest her apprehensions started to fade. Because, on the surface at least, there was here no need for compassion.

Franz Heinz was one of those who had achieved almost every refugee's ambition and had managed to reach the States where he had later taken American nationality. He was a tall, well-built man, as well dressed as Lord Charles himself, and praise could go little higher, with a distinction Lord Charles had never achieved. He had been fortunate enough to be able to put the past behind him, had made a success of his life in the States, and was over on a flying visit on behalf of the company he had helped to found and who wished to establish an English connection. Lord Charles, who looked stupid and was, in fact, rather sharper than the next man, except where cards were concerned, was to meet them later, and give them supper, and there was a reasonable chance that he might be persuaded to make a small but useful investment in the proposed new concern.

" You haven't been waiting long ? " hoped Lady Connie, and he thought in all sincerity that it was worth waiting four times as long for such a hostess. Connie was always quickly recognised and she had hosts of friends and few illusions about her own achievements. " I've been terribly, terribly lucky," she would admit with a candour that endeared her to everyone. And luckiest of all, of course, in meeting and marrying darling Charles.

They drank champagne cocktails. Torquil was right when he said she hardly recognised any other drink. Her escort would have satisfied every captious grandmother, and all went like the proverbial wedding bell until she said in her charming voice, " It's too bad Mr. Luzky couldn't have come. You'd think when he knew another Hungarian would be there . . ." And stopped dead, because if she'd felt a faint cloud over the sun as she drove up the Strand, she was now conscious of something approaching an eclipse.

Franz Heinz turned towards her. " What name was that ? "

" Luzky," she repeated. " Paul Luzky. He was speaking at the Hall . . ."

" It is not possible," returned Franz calmly. " Paul Luzky is dead."

" You mean, someone's told you he's dead ? But it isn't

true. You've been misinformed. Well," as he maintained that curious, disconcerting silence, " a man should know his own name, shouldn't he ? "

" What is he like, this Luzky ? " Franz went on, cool and steady as steel.

She thought a moment. " Did you ever read a book by an English novelist who thought that, as they had every other kind of animal in the Zoo, they ought to have a man as well ? No, I expect not. But if they had, then Mr. Luzky would have been absolutely at home in the bear-pit, those little black bears, you know."

She remembered the man as she spoke, small, compact and dark, with a kind of chilling farouche charm ; and yet —and yet—she, who was never ill-at-ease, hadn't been wholly at ease with him. In some odd way she believed she had felt the sufferings and privations he described so acutely more than he did himself. He's used to it, she had insisted. I come to it fresh, of course I'm shocked. But she remembered, too, her faint yet quite definite sense of relief when he had said he couldn't accept her invitation to come to the Savoy.

Franz, who seemed to have a one-track mind and in a flash was as separated from her as if a door had slammed between them, said, " It is important I should meet this man. You have his address ? "

She shook her head. Everything was happening too fast. At one instant she was enjoying champagne cocktails with one of the most charming and attractive men she had met in a twelvemonth, now he was transformed into an aloof, absorbed machine. If she had turned into stone he would not have noticed, until he found he was getting no replies to his questions.

" The Brigade people would know, but, of course, there won't be anyone at their office this hour of the night. To-morrow . . ."

He sent her a glance that gave her the most unexpected shudder. Not a thrill, nothing apprehensive, but a warning, as if she'd been swimming in shallow water and suddenly when she put her foot down the bottom wasn't there.

" Wait a minute ! " She delved furiously in the ragbag of her mind and came up with a bit of pure glittering gold. " I've just remembered. Something was said about going to a place called the Casbah, a sort of night-club, I suppose. I did think we might all go on. . . ."

She saw his face again and turned an imploring glance on a passing waiter. A telephone book, she whispered. While Franz, whose hands were much steadier than hers, looked for the address, she found her thoughts wandering to a holiday Charles had taken her to Tangier, and the strange atmosphere, like the Old Testament, the laden donkeys, the men in white robes—djibbahs did they call them ?—the ill-assorted animals in the rudimentary ploughs, a camel with a mule or an ox. . . .

Franz's voice brought her back to the present. " The Casbah Coffee Bar. S.W. 5. Would that be it ? "

" I should think it might," she agreed, grasping at reality. " It's the same district. I'll tell you what, bring him back with you—we'll wait. Charles won't be on time anyway, clocks need never have been invented so far as he's concerned, he's like gipsies who tell the time by the stars. . . ."

She saw he wasn't even listening. He had risen to his feet, kissed her hand, thanked her for her hospitality, regretted his abrupt departure and was gone.

" Don't forget, bring him back," she called.

" Who on earth was that, darling ? " She was startled to find someone else at her table. " You look as though you'd just come face to face with your guilty past."

" That was a man called Heinz. He's a refugee. Sit down and keep me company till Charles arrives. I don't know when Mr. Heinz will get back."

He hadn't returned when Lord Charles turned up, an hour late as she had forecast.

" What's happened to your Wog ? " asked Charles.

He was a product of England's most famous public school and though, had Franz been there, no one could have exceeded him in hospitality and charm, he didn't make any secret of the fact that he preferred his room to his company. All men have their blind spots and one of his was a firm belief that every man would have got himself born on a British passport if he'd had the choice.

"He's gone to fetch Mr. Luzky. I told him to bring him back to supper."

"Probably forgotten your existence by now. You know how emotional these foreigners get at reunions."

"That's what's so odd. He didn't look a bit pleased to find his friend wasn't dead, after all."

"Oh well," said Charles, callously, "he probably owes the chap money. Come on, sweetie, they won't turn up now. Settling it with knives, I dare say."

"I wish you wouldn't joke, Charles. I have the feeling that's just what they may be doing."

"We'll leave a message," offered her husband, soothingly. "If either or both turn up they can join us. Foreigners don't care what hour they eat."

But though they stayed at the Savoy till nearly midnight neither Franz nor his presumed compatriot put in an appearance.

: : : :

The man who called himself Paul Luzky sat at a small table at the back of the Casbah with an empty chair opposite him. Since Juliet had fled in and out again, like the famous bird passing through a lighted tent from the dark to the dark, he had scarcely stirred. A bit of a misfit, Jim at the Duck and Daisy had said, and even here he seemed a stranger, in his neat dark suit and collar and tie in a wilderness of pullovers, jerseys, wind-cheaters and the huge shapeless jumpers so many of the girls affected. The place was jam-packed as always ; he'd had difficulty keeping that empty chair ; no weather kept the Casbah clientele at home, the place was like a club. Colour didn't matter here and nor did creed, though age was something else—it was unusual to find anyone over thirty on the premises, and the appearance of a man rising forty and as elegantly turned out as Franz Heinz drew several eyes. Not that they stayed fixed for long. Their owners might have the most casual jobs or no jobs at all, but they contrived to give the impression that the world was theirs and they were just making up their mind what they were going to do with it. Franz Heinz paid off his taxi and made his way through the blue smoky air to the counter. The noise as he pushed the door open assailed him like a blow; then he thought there could be no better place for a rendezvous; you could probably knife a man here without anyone noticing, except the man himself, of course. He bought his cup of coffee and murmured Luzky's name. A slim olive-faced youth indicated the small dark figure sitting hunched in its corner. Franz recalled Lady Connie's description—at home in the bear-pit, she'd said. A clever woman in her way, she'd hit him off to a T. Carrying his cup and threading his way through the sprawled chairs and past the slumped figures on stools by the window, Franz laid a hand on the back of the vacant chair.

"You permit?"

The small dark man looked up; his eyes were sombre as coals.

"I'm expecting a friend."

"Herr Luzky?"

"That's right, though we don't say Herr much over here." His voice lightened a little. "Were you at the meeting to-night?"

"I have just come from the Savoy. Lady Constance told me that Herr Paul Luzky was the speaker, but I knew, of course, she must be wrong. Paul Luzky is dead."

The small dark man put his hand into his breast-pocket and flicked a small document on to the table.

"In that case, it's the first time I've ever known them issue a passport to a ghost."

Franz remained unmoved; he pulled out the chair and sat down.

"What happened to him?" he asked, and there was neither passion nor reproach in his voice. "Was it you?"

"I don't know what you're talking about," insisted the small dark man.

"Paul Luzky. But, of course, I can see you are not the man. Only, I wonder why you are using his name."

"Because it's mine and I've got papers to prove it. Sorry if I don't happen to be your Paul Luzky, if you were so dead keen to meet him—where do you say you came from ?"

" I have come from New York on a business trip. A lady at the Savoy speaks your name . . ."

" And you come beetling over ? Too bad you should have the journey for nothing. Take my word for it, pal, you're wasting your time. Your Paul Luzky isn't going to surface to-night or any night."

" So he is dead ? " the other man insisted.

" In this country no one can be dead without there's a record, a certificate, a gravestone. And take my word for it, you won't find any of those with his name on it. Because he's sitting here, talking to you, the only Paul Luzky you're likely to contact. If he was such a pal of yours, you've been a long time looking him up. He might have died of starvation. . . ."

" That would be too good. The man was a murderer. Because of him forty men died."

" What did he do ? " inquired Paul, curiously. " Chuck a bomb or something ? "

" It was worse than that."

" Such as ? "

" He sold his comrades to the frontier guards in return for his own safe-conduct."

" You mean, you think that's what he did." The small dark man displayed no sign of emotion even now.

" There is no other possible explanation. Listen. You have never, I dare say, lived in a besieged country, I have been away from one so long it is like a dream. The man who lives so is never safe. You know that one day, to-morrow perhaps, they will come for you, probably by night, you will walk up the street, your wife will see you go but she will make no sound, because they are not delicate with women ; perhaps you will see her again, more likely not. So—before that happens you plan to escape, you creep out under cover of darkness, you lie up in the long grass, under the hills, you hug the wire—sometimes you must even hide in the river under the bank. Men have been drowned. . . . And then you make your break for freedom."

"What are you trying to say? That Paul got through and you didn't?"

"All was arranged. There was to be a diversion so that the guards would be taken unawares. You understand?"

"I've seen the films," Paul agreed. "*Wooden Horse* and all that."

"You have seen the films!" For an instant the man who had escaped supported his head on his clasped hands. "But although the diversion went according to plan, they were waiting for us as we broke through. Forty men died that night, others after their return."

"And Paul got clear away? And you think he bought his freedom with a great price like that chap in the Bible? Well, you've no proof, have you? And anyway, it's jungle law. Still, it would explain a lot."

"I do not understand. How did you come to meet such a man?"

"That's simple. Just one of those things. I could very well have chosen another seat on the Embankment, but it so happened I sat on the one where he was. The Embankment's by the river, incidentally, in case you didn't know. I saw some other chap, but I didn't notice him, if you get me, till he asked for a match. Of course, I knew he was a foreigner right away, his voice . . . I pulled out a box and handed it to him. He took out a match and sat there holding it. Then he said, 'If I had a cigarette I could have a smoke.'"

"So you gave him a cigarette?"

"Too right I did. And we got nattering. He told me about getting away from Hungary, same story as yours really, only he didn't cast himself for Judas Iscariot. Someone blew the gaff, he was lucky, eventually got over here and of course was given sanctuary. Only—he was a natural misfit, and of course memories are short and Hungary was a long time ago."

"He asked you for money?"

"Not exactly. Mind you, I didn't take everything he said for gospel, you can't ever trust these winos, and that's what he was when I met him, whatever he may have been in his native land. Easy to see why he couldn't hold down a job. If I hadn't found him that day he'd have been on surgical spirit in three months. And I'll tell you something else, the man was dead scared."

" He had reason to be," returned Heinz in sombre tones.

" Good hater, aren't you ? Like I said, it explains a lot. Why he never went to any of these refugee centres, whatever they're called. Flotsam and jetsam, that was him. Hadn't even got a place to sleep and you know how the bobbies are about moving a chap on. Or perhaps you don't," he added, as an afterthought.

" And so, Mr. . . . ? "

" Call me Paul. It was blowing up for rain and I was going back and I told him he could doss down with me for a night or two, and I knew a chap who might give him a job."

" That was a truly Christian gesture," commented Heinz, ironically.

" Nark it ! I'm not a charitable institution. But a chap I knew was looking for someone, I thought your pal might fit. . . ."

" A man who drank, friendless, without money, pursued by fear—what use could he be ? "

" Say he wanted a bit of backing, a bit of security—only of course he didn't stay the course, or someone didn't let him stay the course."

" You mean, he is dead ? "

" Well, like I told you, he can't be officially dead without a certificate and a gravestone, the lot, but for your peace of mind he won't be troubling you any more."

" How did he die ? "

" A body was taken out of the river Richmond way. Must have been in the water about three weeks. The usual notices went up outside the police stations—Found Drowned—I saw it, and went along, because we were getting a bit concerned about him not turning up, see ? Didn't trouble our heads much the first day or two, these winos sleep where they fall, and he could have been picked up by the police. But he'd been getting jumpier and jumpier, had a letter or two that he destroyed, wouldn't talk, said he wasn't sleeping, said he'd get some stuff from the doctor. But I don't think he ever did. Could have been in touch with a junkie, of course. He'd touched rock bottom before I met him, so if you're harbouring hard thoughts, mister, you can tell yourself he paid his scot all right."

"The life of one traitor against forty patriots?"

Paul shrugged. "Have it your own way. Anyhow, I went along, said I had a brother missing from London, his wife wanted me to take a dekko—it was him all right. Not very pretty after three weeks in the water, but there was this ring they mentioned in the poster, and then he'd got in some sort of accident, lost a top finger-joint. You didn't really notice till he called your attention to it, and it was after he got here, so the Aliens Office wouldn't catch on. And he had a gold tooth he was very proud of. . . ."

This homely detail seemed to reassure Heinz more than all the rest.

"Did you identify him to the police, then?" But his voice was perplexed.

"Oh, be your age," protested Paul, impatiently. "If he was officially dead he couldn't go round speaking for the oppressed, could he? Torquil Holland can do a lot but even he wouldn't try and pull a stunt like setting up a dead man on a platform. No, I told the police the truth. He's not my brother, I said. I did hear later some chap had identified him, though, a fellow called Smith. Said he was his brother-in-law so far as I recall."

"And the police believed him?"

"I dare say he produced some sort of proof. Anyway, the police force in this country is understaffed as it is, they have plenty on their plate without cluttering themselves up with corpses other chaps are ready to take off their hands. I dare say he offered them enough proof to get by. Not my affair."

"And you took his name? That I do not understand."

"Well, it wasn't any good to him any more; and at the time it was convenient to make use of it. If you were thinking of making trouble," he added levelly, "I'd think again. I dare say you're very nicely settled wherever you are, don't want a lot of inconvenient questions asked, and you know what they say about British justice. It 'ud just be your word against his—or mine. Care for a tip, Professor? You go right back where you came from and forget about this Paul Luzky as you've forgotten for the past three years. Sometimes it's cute not to know too much. I've only jollied you along so far because I don't want trouble either. I don't know how they do things in the States, but here the burden of proof's on the chap who brings the accusation. You tell anyone I'm not the real McCoy, and I'll ask you to prove it. Take a dekko at the picture on that passport ? "

" It is not the man I knew."

" What did I tell you ? You're making a mistake, or maybe there were two Paul Luzkys. You say your Paul's dead. Could be you're right. Could be some pal could tell you more about it than I do. Come to think of it, it's funny you should run out on a posh party to look up an old friend you haven't bothered about for three years."

He laughed harshly ; there was no more compassion in him than would cover a pre-war threepenny bit.

Heinz stood up abruptly. " I am content," he said. " But I needed to know."

When he'd taken himself off, the man who called himself Paul Luzky remained crouched over his solitary table, looking more like a little black bear than ever. I always knew this could happen, he thought. Still, not to worry. He won't make trouble. All the same, it mightn't be a bad idea to pull out, in view of Julie's warning. Torquil Holland was a very different proposition. He sat there earnestly making plans for a future that wasn't going to concern him.

He didn't even see Torquil come in. Suddenly there he was, the tall menacing figure in the black turtle-necked sweater and dark trousers, standing where Franz Heinz had stood, equally unfriendly and about forty times as dangerous. Paul had prepared a story about a refugee from the other side of the Berlin wall, but he never had a chance to outline it.

" Well, Jack," Torquil said, and he started uncontrollably, because, whatever he'd been anticipating, it hadn't been that. Torquil pulled out the chair and sat down ; his long leg kicked Paul's brief-case, and Paul held on to it as though it were his life. He was accustomed to taking chances, had been on the windy side of the law for almost as long as he could remember, but to-night everything was happening too fast.

" I'll do the talking," said Torquil, grimly. " And if you don't like what I say we can go to the Aliens Office to-morrow, and I'll repeat it there. I don't say you never knew the genuine article, but I'll wager all I've got you weren't christened Paul. And your father's name wasn't Luzky." Paul said nothing.

Play it cool, he kept telling himself. It isn't always the chap who holds the best cards who wins the rubber, remember.

He heard Torquil out, then he said, " Why are you saying all this to-night ? What's happened to put the wind up you ? Of course I wasn't christened Paul, but you've known that all along."

There was a moment's silence. Then—" You bloody little cheat," said Torquil, softly. " You can't really think you're going to get away with that."

" I don't see why not. We've been getting away with it for more than two years. Yes, I said we. No, this is my turn to have the floor. You go round to your ardent supporters, your tycoons you've persuaded on to the platform, chaps who've pushed you a bit in the Press, and say, ' Well, as a matter of fact, we've been putting on an act but the intentions were good '—what d'you think's going to happen to your Brigade ? And when it makes the general Press, why, you'll be lucky if someone doesn't slap a summons on you. For one thing, who's going to believe you weren't in the know, and for another, even if they did, you're in the position of a tradesman who's expected to guarantee the quality of his goods. You let it be known you've been selling an ersatz line and so far as your precious Brigade is concerned, you've bought it. What's more, you'll be out on your ear from every other society with similar aims. So think twice before you do anything foolish."

"I'd no reason to suppose you were other than genuine," Torquil assured him. "And you might have to answer some pretty embarrassing questions, such as how did you come by Luzky's papers? Thought of that?"

"I got them from you, of course. Everyone knows you go poking that long nose of yours into every international wasps' nest you can locate, I can't think of anyone with a better opportunity to come up with a nice little bit of forgery. Mind you, I don't want trouble, but if you mean to make it, I'll meet you. The *Daily Screech* 'ud pay a packet for the yarn the way I'd tell it. It couldn't have come at a better time, really. Lady Connie's always news, probably put up my price."

"I believe you'd do it," said Torquil slowly. "The Brigade doesn't mean a thing to you."

"Be your age, Holland. I'm like everyone else, I live in a jungle and I get my meat the best way I know. Now, listen. I'll give you till midday to think things over. Naturally, if I don't get my killing from the Press, I'll have to be compensated on some scale."

"Blackmail, too!" murmured Torquil. He spoke quite softly, and there was a good deal of noise going on all round them, but even so a few of those nearest half-turned, stiffening at the sound of his voice; and remembered it afterwards. A wiser man than Paul might have reckoned this was the time to pull out, and not return.

"I'll leave you to think things over," the little dark man went on. "I've got to do a bit of telephoning now—I don't think I'll use the phone on the stairs, it's a bit public. So long, and don't do anything I wouldn't do."

He picked up his brief-case and was gone before Torquil could acclimatise himself to this astounding turning of tables. He sat for a moment like a black statue, then, as if a penny had dropped with a resounding clang, he pushed his chair back with such violence he overturned the untouched cup of coffee.

He didn't stop to clear up the mess or even to apologise for making it, possibly he didn't even notice. He was aware of nothing but a searing fury against the man he'd known as Paul Luzky and a determination to stop him making yet more mischief. He stood outside the Casbah for a moment, trying to pierce the curtain of fog. A modern sculptor might have reduced him to a stark figure, stiff as ice, dark as the night. Then he turned and disappeared. As he went he caught sight of a clock in a neighbouring shop window. It said 10.40.

It was staggering to realise he'd only been in the Casbah for ten minutes.

CHAPTER III

MR. CROOK STAYED at the Duck and Daisy till closing-time. The fog hadn't diminished, but that didn't worry him. Almost opposite the end of the Brandon Passage was a bus stop, and as he approached it one of four or five people waiting there detached himself and came towards him.

"Mr. Crook?" he said in a low voice. "I've been waiting for you. I went round to your place but it was all dark, so I guessed you'd be coming along any time now. I'm in trouble, Mr. Crook."

"If ever I find a time when you're not I'll eat my hat," said Crook, cheerfully. "Now look, Harry, I can't discuss business at this hour. I've got an office. . . ."

"They'll be watching that," said Harry. "Honest, Mr. Crook, they've got it wrong. I don't know no more about this break-in than a babe unborn."

"Some of these new-born kids should have their heads examined," was Crook's unsympathetic reply. "How's it going to help your pals if I get gated for perjury?"

"I was home with Lulu, honest I was, but you know what the slops are. They don't take a wife's word. Well, if I was all they think I am, wouldn't she want me to be put away?"

"Don't ask me," said Crook. "I'm not married."

Harry grinned. Even in the poor visibility his teeth shone like tombstones. "Can't see you on the ball-and-chain," he admitted. "What I want to know is will you act for me? They can't make you talk not without you've got a lawyer—though come to that, some of these rozzers don't know as much about the law as the poor bleeders they pick up."

"Here comes your bus," said Crook, unemotionally, as the monster panted up through the fog.

"It'll mean P.D. for me this time, you know that."

"Pity you didn't think of it earlier," said Crook, unsympathetically. "I warned you before it was time you thought of settling down."

"Ten quid a week and spend my nights watching the telly? Strewth, Mr. Crook, I might as well be in the grave."

"I haven't time to listen to the rest of your life-story to-night," Crook assured him, pleasantly. "Go on, that's the last long-distance bus running before morning. And if you do decide you need me you've got my number. But just remember I'm a lawyer, not a miracle-worker."

"You try telling that to the boys, Mr. Crook. Ta a million." And Mr. Morgan hopped on the bus and ran up the steps, as gaily as if his acquittal was already in the bag.

When the bus had departed, taking with it Mr. Harry Morgan on what might be his last bus-ride for about eight years, Crook crossed the road and turned into the passage. It seemed to him darker than it had been only a few minutes before, and when he reached the kiosk he realised why. Someone had kicked over the warning red light while the box itself was in darkness. He supposed it was possible for the bulb to have conked out, but it was much more likely that some hooligan had smashed it by way of a joke—some of these chaps had the most primitive sense of humour—or (and this was his bet) it had been removed by a courting couple who didn't see why they should give the passer-by a free entertainment. He realised as he came closer that the box was occupied. In the red lamp's uncertain beam he could make out two figures in what appeared to be a pretty affectionate embrace. But the narrowness of the passage, the disposal of the lamp, and the steadily thickening fog obliterated everything in the way of detail. He thought they must be pretty far gone to come all this way in such weather just to snog in a telephone kiosk. Still, none of his business, or so he assumed at the time. He stamped past—neither of them paid him the least attention—and moved into the narrow alley that led into Brandon Street. As he turned the second corner to find himself four doors from his own home he heard footsteps going softly away from the kiosk through the fog. He frowned as he fitted his key into the door as if something bothered him, but when he was on the mat he could hear a telephone shrilling away a long way off.

" Can't be mine," he thought, but because this might be his evening for miracles he went bouncing up the stairs like a big brown rubber ball, and when he reached the top there was the bell still sending out its signal. He rushed in and snatched the receiver from the hook. A cheerful male voice said, " Number, please ? " and he gave it without stopping to think.

" Just testing the line," said the engineer, and all the warmth of the Orient swam into Crook's cheerful voice as he exclaimed, " That's what I call service. Why, I only reported this on my way out to the Duck and Daisy."

" Can't afford to have you off the air, Mr. Crook," said the engineer, who was clearly a waggish type. " Never know when we mightn't be wanting you ourselves."

The line went dead again and a hideous green marble clock on the mantelpiece, the gift of a grateful client, started to chime eleven. Five minutes behind time just like its donor.

" If I'd waited a couple of hours I could have made the call from my own number," Crook reflected. And then he remembered how his skin had tingled and felt sure there was some purpose in it, after all. But all the same he wasn't wholly at ease. Something nagged to which he couldn't put a name, some trifle he'd overlooked, something that perhaps constituted a clue to a mystery waiting round the corner. He opened another bottle of beer in case that brought inspiration, but it didn't, and he went to bed with his problem unsolved. By the time he woke a good many things had happened that were going to affect him, but even if he had known that he wouldn't have worried, because that sort of thing was happening all the time, and when it stopped happening there'd be nothing ahead but the grave.

: : : :

But this evening, that was to have fatal consequences for more than one party concerned, was not yet over. Just as Crook was pouring out his final bottle of beer and starting to think how to twist the law's arm on Harry Morgan's behalf, a man called Fenner came up the steps of Brandon Street Underground Station. He was returning from an evening at the dogs, and he stopped before stepping into the street, partly to light a cigarette, and partly to accustom his eyes to the gloom. He was tossing the match away when someone came lurching round the corner from the direction of the passage. Fenner's first notion was that the new-comer had had a few, and the next that he didn't know if he was on terra firma or hanging between earth and heaven. Fenner, who had experience of both states, came forward a step to inquire impulsively, " You all right, mate ? " At first the chap didn't seem to have heard him, then he turned his head like a mechanical man.

" Yes," he said, " of course I'm all right. This damned fog. Can't see your hand before your face." And then he asked if there was an underground station nearby.

" Why, you're standing in it, or as near as makes no difference. Here, what's wrong ? " (Later he was to tell the police, " I thought he was loco, he seemed to be looking right through me, and he just stood like that woman in the Bible who was turned into salt.")

" Hold up, mate. D'you want a doctor ? " Fenner asked, and at that the man did come to life ; he swerved away from the hand the dog-follower automatically stretched out towards him, and the movement brought him into the circle of light at the station's mouth. He muttered something about a taxi.

"You won't find many of them cruising around a night like this," Fenner warned him. "There was one but some other chap got it. You'd do better to take the train, and no slower, believe me." Then his voice changed abruptly. "Good God, what's that?"

His eyes were fixed on a large dark stain on the front of the stranger's coat.

"You been having a barney?" he demanded. "Maybe you do want a doctor after all."

The stranger with a sudden gesture freed himself from the tentative hand on his arm. "Nothing to worry about," he muttered. "Practical joke. Just red paint."

"Paint be blowed," Fenner exclaimed, his ears agog for the sound of following feet. A married man, with two kiddies, he didn't want to get mixed up in one of these gang feuds. But, except for the pair of them, the world seemed deserted. Before he could say anything else, his companion had thrust past him and was clattering down the steps. Fenner saw him push a coin into an automatic machine and grab the ticket. He shrugged. Oh well, chaps never said thank you for interference, and no man who could move at that pace was going to die on his feet. Probably he'd been at a party, they'd all had a few drinks, someone had started shoving around and there'd been a bit of claret-tapping—anyway, not to worry and not his show, and he had troubles of his own. He had to explain to his wife how it was he'd forgotten his promise to take her to the pictures; and then he saw his bus, which wasn't the same number as the one Harry Morgan had taken, grunting like some prehistoric beast through the fog, so he dived across the road and ran up the steps. For no particular reason he glanced at the watch on his wrist. It was 11.25.

And it was about twenty minutes after that that Lady Connie murmured reluctantly something about a television rehearsal next day, and the party broke up. The chauffeur, Benson, said they got back to the immense luxury flat in Carisbrooke House just at midnight. Connie, to whom to think was to act, hurried along to find a brooch of yellow diamonds she intended to give to the Peace Brigade funds, while Lord Charles mixed a nightcap for them both.

"Plain soda for me," said Lady Connie, but it looked so pale he was just brightening it a bit from his own bottle when he heard a cry.

"What's up?" asked Lord Charles, jerking rather more whisky into his own glass than he'd intended. "House been burgled?"

He nearly dropped the bottle itself when she said "Yes."

It was a very neat job, the police told her later, a professional job. There'd been a big party in the flat above, so no one would notice a stranger, and, since she had been careful to wear the minimum of jewellery for the meeting, the thief or thieves had made a pretty good killing.

The insurance value of the missing jewellery was £15,000.

: : : :

So—good-bye, Friday, roll on, Saturday, and an eventful Saturday it was going to be. It started, so far as the little clique involved with the mysterious Paul Luzky was concerned, at 2.30 a.m., when P.C. Wain, a recent recruit to the Metropolitan Force, patrolling down Manders Street, which ran past the far end of Brandon Passage, felt an overwhelming desire for a cigarette. The fog was still thick, and the atmosphere like a damp yellow blanket. Apart from himself, the world seemed deserted. Even the traffic to-night travelled by the main road. P.C. Wain dodged into the mouth of Brandon Passage, walked a little distance to make certain that, even in this fog, he couldn't be recognised, and struck a match. Drawing luxuriously on the fag he moved a few steps along the passage, and that was how he came to realise that there was no light in the telephone kiosk. He thought, as Crook had done, it had probably been removed by a couple who preferred the dark, and decided he'd best replace it. He nearly fell over a loose brick as he approached the box, and stooped to right the fallen red lamp.

"Might have broken my ankle. Why can't these chaps

clear things up before they go off ? " he asked of the fog, that couldn't have cared less.

He pulled open the door and shone his bull's-eye into the interior of the booth, and then for a moment a wave of green sickness overcame him. It should be remembered that he was young, inexperienced, the weather conditions were unpropitious, and it so happened that never before had he seen a dead person. And this man was very, very dead. He had clearly been attacked from behind, probably while he was getting a number or even while he was speaking, though in that case you might have expected his correspondent to give the alarm when the conversation was abruptly terminated. So perhaps he hadn't succeeded in making contact. The weapon was the familiar blunt instrument, quite probably one of the bricks that scattered the path, to judge from the untidy nature of the wound. All P.C. Wain could see was that the dead man was shortish and dark. The cigarette, that had dropped from the constable's mouth, glowed from the paving-stones, and automatically he set his foot on it. Then carefully he shut the door and made a bee-line for the underground station where he shut himself into a telephone box and rang his sergeant.

"You're sure he's dead, not just drink taken ? " barked the official voice.

P.C. Wain gulped. " Yes, sir, he's dead all right. The back of his head . . ."

" All right, all right. Now get back right away, we don't want any interference with the body. We'll be along in a brace of shakes, and—get this, Wain—don't touch anything and detain anyone who turns up and shows any interest in it. You won't have to wait long, and remember—*don't touch anything*."

P.C. Wain didn't obey this instruction to the letter, because, examining the site as best he could, he noticed the crushed cigarette end and hurriedly dealt with it by putting it in his pocket. Ambitious young policemen don't make the grade by letting their superior officers realise their misdemeanours, even trivial ones, why, he might even find himself held for laying false clues. He tried to remember if he'd heard any footsteps as he came down the alley but he was pretty sure he hadn't, though the fog would muffle all sounds. Fragments of the smashed bulb were scattered on the floor of the booth; others were embedded in the extensive red wound.

It seemed a long time, though actually it was only a matter of minutes, before he heard footsteps and the place seemed suddenly full of people. They'd brought a doctor along, who said death must have been practically instantaneous, and in his opinion two blows had been struck. The weapon was most likely a brick or part of a brick, and as the wall had been more or less demolished at this spot, there were plenty of those. The crime, in his opinion, had been committed not earlier than ten o'clock or later than midnight.

Inspector Oakapple, who was in charge, said gloomily, "This is going to be a honey from our point of view. Even if anyone heard footsteps who's going to risk identification in this weather? Not likely to be any witnesses hanging around, I'd say the chap never knew what hit him, and he can't have realised his danger or he wouldn't have come to an out-of-the-way place like this. Don't know what the authorities wanted to put a kiosk here for anyway."

(The same thought had occurred to Crook, but he had decided in his slapdash way that they were probably hand in glove with the Vice Brigade.)

"Must have followed his man into the alley," pursued Inspector Oakapple. "Waited till he started dialling and then —wham! Any trace of brick-dust in the wound, Doctor?"

"Oh, it was a brick all right," the doctor agreed. He looked round him. "Well, chap could take his pick. You might call it putting temptation in a man's path."

"The adult population," retorted Oakapple, dryly, "is supposed to be educated to resist temptation. Whatever the motive it wasn't robbery. He's got a nice fat wallet in his pocket and a nice heavy gold watch on his wrist. But no letters, no cards, nothing to indicate who he is."

"I'll tell you something," said the doctor. "The chap who did this must bear traces of blood, quite noticeable traces. You can't commit this kind of murder by remote control. Unless, of course, you're anticipating one of these naked murderer cases, which somehow doesn't seem very probable."

"Where does a wise man hide a leaf?" muttered Oakapple. "Even if we can identify the actual brick it's not likely to do us much good. And it doesn't really prove anything—that it was an unpremeditated crime, say. Because he might have brought a weapon along and then seen the brick and decided to use that instead."

He told Wain to go back to his duties and keep his eyes peeled.

"We'll have a man each end of the passage and keep the way clear. Better have a third man in the passage itself, in case X comes sneaking through the alley."

Not that he anticipated much movement on such a night, unless that undependable fellow, Arthur Crook, was on the rampage, and he'd put nothing past him.

The Press came out with a statement the next morning. The dead man was described as being aged 30-32, dark of hair and eyes, clean-shaved, height slightly below average. Nothing special about his get-up, everything very correct and dark and impersonal. No special physical characteristics like a club foot or facial scars. But a few million people would read the account in the papers and one of them might come forward with a story of a husband or son or lodger who hadn't returned last night.

"One of these days," suggested Pressman A to Pressman B, "the police 'ull really get cracking, and we shall find the murderer of the body in the box was the rozzer who found it."

"That'll be the day," agreed Pressman B as they rushed off to telephone their respective papers.

CHAPTER IV

THE FOG BLEW away during the night. When Crook opened his eyes he saw as bright a day as you could wish for. The fog also seemed to have dispersed from his brain and he knew at once what it was that had perplexed him the previous evening. When he passed the telephone booth he had seen two people inside; they were no more than shadows but he'd have staked his davy there were two of them. Yet only *one* set of footsteps had gone away down the passage. He didn't try and convince himself that the other half of the couple had stayed behind to telephone; you don't telephone from a pitch-dark kiosk. No, something was in the wind, and as soon as he opened his paper—he took four, all of the gossip column variety, leaving world problems to those better able to cope with them—he knew what it was. The body of a man not yet identified and with fatal head injuries had been found in a telephone booth in a passage in London, S.W. 5.

"Could be anyone," reflected Crook, gloomily, feeling he'd been double-crossed—so near and yet so far, a miss is as good as a mile, all his favourite clichés came rushing through his head like dogs after the electric hare. He reached for his telephone and called his A.D.C., Bill Parsons. "Might be a bit late," he said, "and get the gen on Harry Morgan." In his notorious yellow Rolls, known to himself as the Old Superb and to less reverent chaps as the Ancient of Days, he tooled up to the handsome sub-police station near the High Street, where his mere appearance attracted instant attention. He never fooled himself that he was their favourite man, but he did quite frankly expect them to run up a flag when he turned up to give them a hand, even if it was only the Jolly Roger.

"This chap in the phone box," began Crook, and they passed him on gratefully to Inspector Oakapple.

" Can't help wondering what the murderer thought when he heard your number ten feet come up the alley," mused Oakapple.

" He was safe enough," Crook retorted. " I can be as nosy as the next man, but I was never called Peeping Tom."

" Didn't get a glimpse of either of them, of course." It was a statement, not a question: the inspector doodled rapidly.

Crook shook his head. If this had been his office in Bloomsbury Street there'd have been beer to sweeten the conversation, but rozzers do have to work under disadvantages, you must hand them that.

" I thought they were a couple of doves, the kind that prefer the dark." He did a rapid imitation of a pair of turtle-doves and even the inspector looked startled. " I wasn't to know one of them had coo-ed for the last time," Crook explained, quite without rancour. But, though he seemed placid enough, he was inwardly shaken that that sixth sense on which he depended shouldn't have warned him that murder was in the wind.

" Well, that fixes the time at 11," the inspector said. " Fits in with the doctor's ideas, too. Yes, Hyde ? "

For a sergeant had knocked and opened the door.

" There's a Mrs. Hart here, sir. She's a landlady from Cook Street, and she's got a lodger who never turned up last night. Answers the description, more or less."

" And that surprises her ? " questioned the inspector, cynically. " How long's she been a landlady ?"

" She said it never happened before and he was a man with enemies, a foreigner by all accounts. Name of Luzky."

" What's that ? " exclaimed Crook, jumping into the air as if he had sat on a darning-needle.

"L-U-Z-K-Y," repeated the sergeant.

" Don't tell me his first name was Paul."

The inspector groaned. " We might have known." Murder was quite enough of a headache as it was, without Crook coming along to tangle everything up. The simplest case turned into a Laocoön-like design when that great red head and those brown popping eyes came pushing into it.

"He does public speaking for these refugees," the sergeant went on. "He's one himself. Hungarian," he elaborated.

Crook made it clear from the start he was going to make everything as difficult as possible.

"That's what you think," he retorted.

"And you don't, Mr. Crook?"

"Why ask me? I never set eyes on the chap, to my knowledge. But there's a group of young people who call themselves the Peace Brigade or something of the sort, who have their doubts."

And he went into a spiel about the conversation he'd overheard the previous evening at the Duck and Daisy.

"Health Service should give you a medal," said the inspector. "You'll never trouble them for a hearing-aid."

"There was some talk of going along to the Casbah," offered Crook mildly. "No, I didn't trail along. For one thing, no one was paying me to be nosy, for another I ain't teetotal. Lastly, it sounds like the kind of place where you're expected to leave your shoes on the mat, and I stopped going round barefoot about forty years ago."

The sergeant went away to prepare Mrs. Hart for a visit to the mortuary, and Oakapple suggested Crook might like to go along, too.

"Viewing stiffs isn't my idea of a good Saturday morning's fun," said Crook, who, after more than thirty years, could never quite achieve indifference in the presence of something that so short a time before had been alive and was now violently jolted out of existence. He realised what the inspector was thinking—you know such a lot of rummies you might know this one as well, seeing he's not the Hungarian refugee he claims. Crook shrugged. "Have it your own way," he said, "but don't expect me to help you. I'm a Union Jack man myself."

When Mrs. Hart saw the body she indulged in a mild attack of hysterics, though it presented a much tidier appearance now than when the unfortunate constable had nearly fallen over it some hours before.

" That's him," she said. " I warned him."

" Against whom ? "

She stared. " Them, of course. Coming from abroad the way he did and always talking against Them, well, it stands to reason they'd get him if they could."

The police sergeant tried to sort this incoherence into some kind of order.

" Did he have any definite threats ? Did he ever mention a name ? "

" They never know the names," returned the woman, darkly. " It's all part of the System. You ought to ask for police protection, I told him—that's when he had a phone call at my house and came away looking ever so queer. This is a free country, I told him, not like the one you've been lucky enough to leave behind, and any man here has a right to speak his mind, not that I agree with all these foreigners coming over, mark you, if they'd been meant to settle here they'd have been born British, wouldn't they ? "

No one picked up that gauntlet.

" I understand he used to appeal for funds for the refugees," said Sergeant Hyde. " He must have left Hungary a long time ago. It's hardly likely they'd be after him still."

" It's the Reds," declared Mrs. Hart, with no intention of being done out of her moment of the limelight. " They're like bugs. Get them in the wall and you can fumigate and fumigate, but they'll go on coming back. Only way to be sure of getting rid of them for good is pull the house down." She repeated. " No, you mark my words, They were after him and They got him."

Crook passed her as the patient officer led her away, and went to stand by the slab where the dead man was lying. It was not a particularly pleasant face, dark and harsh, and it looked even more dead than corpses generally do, perhaps because the only other time Crook had seen it it had been alight with purposeful malice.

" Well, Mr. Crook ? " asked the man at his side, after the pause seemed to him to have gone on long enough.

"Well, I can tell you who he is," said Crook, slowly, "but it's only substituting one headache for another. That chap there—he was wearing a silly little moustache last time I saw him, say about three years ago, the kind of thing his type hangs on to while pulling themselves up by their boot-straps—is Jack Aslett. You don't recognise the name? Well, I dare say he used more than one. But he was never more than a small-time operator. Shady little con. man jobs, blackmailing in a small way. Spot of smash and grab mightn't come amiss. I came across him when he was fleecing an old girl on account of some silly letters her daughter had written. She had the sense to come to me, most of them don't."

"Seems a biggish jump from that to speaking in public for refugees."

"You can be sure there's something in it for Walter, and you clever chaps will be able to puzzle it out."

"That wasn't what you meant when you spoke of a headache?" the police officer hazarded.

"No. In fact—no. Y'see, that Brides-in-the-bath chap was right when he said when they're dead they're finished. Meaning they don't rise from a watery grave after two years to get themselves killed all over again in a telephone box in S.W. 5. And according to official records, a chap called Jack Aslett was taken out of the river near Richmond, Surrey, about two years ago."

: : : :

"Well, of course," said Oakapple, "what else did you expect with Crook in the field? Who was the chap who put in a thumb and pulled out a plum? Crook's fingers are all thumbs."

Goodness knew, murder gave you trouble enough when it was, so to speak, straightforward, but when you had a corpse who had been impersonating someone else, who also died in mysterious circumstances—no actual suggestion of foul play in the earlier case, but chaps have to get into the water somehow and they can be shoved just as easily as pole-axed—that was enough to make any policeman's head go round like a teetotum.

It was symptomatic that it didn't occur to him that Crook's identification might be wrong.

Crook, who kept records of everyone who swam into his ken, which might explain the fact that his office appeared to offer less and less sitting-space for his clients, could supply chapter and verse regarding the late alleged Jack Aslett. He had, according to medical opinion, been in the water for about a month.

If anybody had missed him it hadn't been to the extent of making inquiries of the police. There had been little enough by way of identification, just a rather remarkable heavy gold ring and a missing finger-joint. The usual notices FOUND DROWNED appeared outside the police stations, and the usual folk turned up, wanting to trace some relative they perhaps hadn't seen for years, but now desired to contact, mostly for some financial reason. No one could put a name to the fellow, though, until a chap called Walter Smith came down from the north. He'd been visiting in London, he explained, and he'd seen the poster. The mention of the ring and the missing finger-joint made him think it might be his brother-in-law, whom they hadn't set eyes on for more than two years. He identified the ring and he also spoke of a gold tooth, and sure enough there was a gold tooth in the skull. There seemed no ulterior reason why anyone should want the corpse for some form of skulduggery, and it was duly handed over. Aslett was described by his brother-in-law as a bachelor and there was no record of any marriage in that name that could apply to the dead man. So Smith got permission to have the poor wretch coffined and buried decently, though hardly extravagantly, and the page was turned.

And now here was Crook upsetting all the tidy official records declaring that someone had blundered. Efforts to trace Walter Smith would naturally be made, though it was all Lombard Street to a china orange that he wasn't using his right name, not if there was anything fishy about the identification, and there was no blinking the fact that Paul Luzky the refugee had only surfaced, so far as the public was concerned, after the body had been found in the river.

Crook, who wasn't hampered as the authorities are by a need to produce chapter and verse for his conclusions, was instantly convinced that the body found in the river was that of the unfortunate Luzky. The interesting part of the problem was why Aslett should want to take on so colourless (and apparently impoverished) a personality, when, according to police records, no one was looking for him.

Still (so ran Crook's thoughts) Mrs. Hart had a point when she said *They* were a man's worst enemies. Maybe he'd done a bit of double-crossing in his time, using another moniker. It's part of the English heritage to pour scepticism on the idea that anyone born with a British passport would want to pass himself off as an alien. " And," Crook decided, " Aslett must have known the dead man, because he's been putting up quite a good show for the past two years, and who could have given him the gen except someone who'd come over from the trouble-spot ? "

Still, no skin off his nose, and he popped out and into the Old Superb. Mrs. Hart, recovered now from her mild fit of hysterics, was standing on the pavement and he offered her a lift. But she said a murder in the house was bad enough, you didn't want to aggravate it by looking a figure of fun and she hurried away, adding, " This kind of thing doesn't do me any good, you know."

" Hasn't done him much good either," Crook reminded her, and, having for once obtained the female prerogative of the last word, he shot away.

:: ::

Fenner saw the news on the front page of the *Morning Sun*, and knew at once he'd been talking to the murderer. You didn't have to be a rozzer to tie up a man with blood all over his coat with a newly-killed body in a phone box fifty yards away.

" Here, Bess," he called to his wife. " Listen to this." He read the paragraph.

" Don't know what you want to get so excited about," said Bess grumpily. " You didn't do him in, I suppose ? "

He said simply, " If I had murder in mind I'd look a bit

nearer home. But—listen, Bess—I talked to the chap who did."

She remained unimpressed, as only a wife could. " And he told you all about it ? Whatever made him do that ? Now, listen to me, Tom Fenner. You're not going to get yourself mixed up in this. Murder's low and you've got the kids to think of. And if you think I'm going to have the police calling here—goodness knows, the neighbourhood's cheesy enough. . . ."

" According to you, if it was any lower it 'ud be on the sea-bed. Look, girl, you don't understand. This is murder."

" And what do you suppose you can do ? Would you recognise this man again ? "

" In a fog like last night's ? Be your age, girl."

" So how can you help ? Might even identify the wrong man, we all know what the police are like, or they'd start having funny ideas about you."

She went on like this till he said, " O.K., play it your way. But if I get taken for accessory and you and the kids have to go on National Assistance, never say I didn't warn you."

The police, meanwhile, were baying after the criminal as loud as any pack of doberman pinschers. Acting on information received (from Arthur Crook) they went first to the Casbah, but that wasn't open and no one seemed to live on the premises, so they swept round to the headquarters of the Peace Brigade. Here they were more fortunate. In the one basement room in Battersea that comprised their offices, Inspector Oakapple found Rupert Bowen and the dark girl called Ruth. But of the man calling himself Paul Luzky there was no sign.

" Expecting him this morning ? " the police inquired.

" Care to declare an interest ? " murmured Rupert.

" I'm asking you if you're expecting him, sir."

" Well, he usually does turn up on Saturdays. It's fairly early yet and we're inclined to go in shifts. Miss Danesfoot and I are the first shift and then Juliet Ware and Paul come on, and the others take over from them. Sometimes in the afternoon there are several of us here, because that's when we get the most inquiries, and it's a chance for us all to get together and plan the next step."

"He hasn't rung you, sent a message?"

Rupert shook his head.

"What do you want with him?" he asked, curiously. "He hasn't been slipping his hand in a church collecting box or anything? O.K., only my joke, but when the boys in blue start assembling you do tend to look round for your life-jacket."

Oakapple let him have it, both barrels. "We've reason to believe he's the man whose body was found in the telephone box in Brandon Passage. You've seen the papers?"

"I saw it," agreed Ruth. She had turned very pale. "Why should you suppose . . . ?"

"His landlady reported he hadn't come home last night, and she identified him at the mortuary."

"Good God!" said Rupert, simply. "Who did it? Not old Torquil?"

"Of course it wasn't Torquil," cried Ruth in a voice that was almost a shout. "Do think what you're saying. This may be a thrill for you, but these are the police."

"This Torquil," began the inspector, and they both hastened to explain he was the one who started the movement five years ago.

"We're fairly small beer, I suppose," Rupert acknowledged, "but at least the flavour's good. We have a branch in the north and what you might call sympathisers in other places. They help to arrange meetings and put up the speakers—you know."

"Mr. Holland," amplified Ruth, "is really the backbone of the party. The rest of us have jobs to get on with and can only give our spare time, but he goes all over the place, Europe, Asia, anywhere to get the story."

"Pressman?" inquired Oakapple, laconically.

"It's more all things to all men," explained Rupert. The fellow certainly had his gang rooting for him, Oakapple decided. "He has written articles, but only as a freelance and no lance was ever freer," he added, with a sudden grin that made him look no more than twenty or twenty-one.

"Was he the one that got hold of Mr. Luzky ?"

They explained together that Torquil had been out of the country when Paul surfaced, that he'd got a temporary job behind Jim's bar. "And Jim wasn't sorry to hand him over to us," said Ruth, frankly. "And I suppose it's only fair to add that he was pretty useful. Till he came we couldn't keep the office open all day, and if sympathisers turn up and find the door locked they never seem to use their heads. They say, 'Oh, perhaps they've shut down.'..."

"Or take it as a personal insult," agreed Rupert. "'Look at me, I've come all this way to offer my sympathy'—some of them went further, they were prepared to address envelopes, which, after all, none of us ever wanted to do——"

Oakapple had his own views about people who were prepared to address envelopes, but he only said, "And since this Luzky fellow appeared you could keep the place open all day ?"

"We did wonder how he lived on what we could afford to pay," Rupert acknowledged, and Ruth broke in: "Well, in a sense, you could say we were playing his game for him. I mean, he was a refugee—at least, that's what we thought at the time, now it seems probable he isn't, in which case—Inspector, why did he put up this elaborate façade ? You must have some idea. It can't have been for the money, because we didn't really pay him a living wage, we explained about that, but he said it was all right he could make it up by working in the evening. He used to go out as a spare waiter, there was nothing haughty about him...."

"Foreigners always seem able to wait," Rupert agreed. "Like Americans, perhaps, who, one hears, help to work themselves through college in the vacations."

Oakapple asked curiously, "Do either of you remember the war ?" and the man said at once: "I did my National Service overseas. Not even Torquil was old enough to fight, and he can give us about three years. And the girls were only born about the time of Munich."

" Of course. What first gave you the idea Luzky might be—well, not what he represented himself ? "

" Nothing very definite. It wasn't like a flash of lightning, I mean he didn't drop one tremendous brick through the roof, so that everyone saw stars, it was like that chap, Arthur Hugh Clough." Oakapple gaped. They bobbed about like ducklings on the Serpentine on a windy day. " You know, through creeks and inlets making, comes silent, flooding in, the main. Place names seem to leave him absolutely fogged, and you don't forget so easily even after five years or so, not if you were past twenty at the time of the Revolution, and I'd say he was thirty or more, wouldn't you, Ruth ? "

" I'm hopeless at ages," murmured Ruth vaguely, " but yes, something like that. I didn't actually suspect him myself, and you never said a word," she added accusingly, to Rupert.

" I'm nobbut the cabin-boy," he reminded her. " And I felt, if there was anything wrong, Torquil would be bound to notice. The trouble with him is he's always living in the middle of next week. On his death-bed he'll be speculating what he'll be doing while the rest of us are queueing up at his funeral."

" According to him, he had suspicions for some time," recalled Ruth, " but he only spoke about them last night. He said he was going to have it out with Paul, which is why Julie—Miss Ware, she should be along any minute and you can ask her yourself—said she was going to the Casbah to warn him."

" Does anyone know if she saw him ? "

" We haven't seen her," Rupert began, but Ruth broke in : " Yes, she did. I left my Jacqmar—my scarf," she added, explanatorily, " at the little flea-pit, and I thought as she more or less passed the door on the way here perhaps she'd drop in and ask if it had been found. Not that I feel very optimistic."

" And she told you . . . ? "

" Not then. I didn't speak to her last night, the landlady said she was washing her hair, it's a pay phone there, and the woman seemed rather offended at being rung up so late—I suppose it'd be about eleven o'clock . . . or a few minutes after."

" Late ? " murmured Rupert, sounding scandalised.

" Well, for her, I suppose. But I got through to Julie this morning and she said she had told Paul. She said she didn't think it made any difference, whatever that may mean."

" You can ask her yourself," said Rupert, quickly. " Here she comes."

Juliet came in, carrying a black and red scarf.

" Your lucky day, Ruth ! I didn't see . . ."

" This is a police inspector," Rupert said, and she stood quite stiff.

" For us ? " she asked. " What's happened ? "

" Should anything have happened ? " the inspector inquired.

" Well, we don't generally get them here. Of course, if there's a demonstration, like the time we massed outside that embassy . . ."

When she heard the news she looked as if she couldn't believe it.

" Paul dead ? I can't take it in. He was all right last night. I don't think he quite believed me when I told him Torquil had discovered he wasn't a Hungarian after all."

" You mean, he suspected his bona fides," Oakapple suggested.

" Oh, no. Mr. Holland wouldn't have said what he did, if he hadn't been sure. He's a very accurate kind of person. He hated even small errors, he said they were the sign of a slovenly mind."

" What time was it when you last saw him, Miss Ware ? "

" I went straight from the Duck and Daisy, I don't think I looked at my watch. It must have been a bit after ten, I suppose. When I got to the Casbah I thought at first he hadn't arrived, then he came through from the back where he'd been telephoning—there's a coin box on the stairs."

" How did he take what you'd come to tell him ? "

" It was queer, he didn't seem to think it was terribly important. He said, ' I'll sort it out with him when he turns up.' And then something about Torquil always having a bee in his bonnet."

" He didn't give any hint as to who he'd been talking to? "

" No. It wasn't any concern of mine."

" Miss Ware," said Oakapple, " this is very important. Did he seem shocked or indignant or treat it as an absurd joke—did he even seem surprised ? "

" He said, ' Leave this to me, I'll sort it out with him,' meaning Torquil Holland. No, he certainly wasn't amused or—or staggered. I got the impression he was so deeply involved in whatever he'd been doing—he'd told us he was making a fresh contact—I thought he hardly took in what I said. Wasn't he making a fresh contact or was that part of the play-acting ? "

" He was making a fresh contact all right," said Ruth, unexpectedly. " I didn't see him to speak to, but when I went back *en route* for my flea-pit I saw him through the glass of the Casbah. He was sitting at a table talking to a man I'd never met before, rather an embassy official type, I'd have said."

" You don't even know if Mr. Holland saw him ? Well, he'll be able to tell me that himself. What time did he leave you after last night's meeting ?—Paul Luzky, I mean."

" He went a bit early," Rupert recalled. " It didn't surprise us, because we knew he'd already refused to go on to the Savoy with Lady Connie, he said he had to meet a man, but we were to look out for him at the Casbah. He left after his own speech, a little before nine, I should think."

" What I don't understand," said Ruth, "is what he was doing with our mob at all, if he wasn't a refugee. I mean, what was in it for him ? Not money, he must have lived from hand to mouth on what we could pay, and I don't suppose his evening jobs were all that remunerative. . . ."

" You're riding in front of the hounds, sweetie," Rupert murmured. " The inspector's been picking our brains ever since he arrived, but he hasn't put any cards on the table himself. Do you know who he was, Inspector ?"

"We've been given an identification," acknowledged Oakapple. "Naturally, we shall require proof, but—did you say he was the one who did the home visiting ?"

"That's right. Actually, I believe he was the one who suggested it. It was all right so long as we had some sort of introduction—Torquil could pull quite a lot of strings, but after some years the supply runs out, and then you have to send requests into the blue. . . ."

"Did he visit Lady Constance before the meeting ?"

"He did. He didn't do things by halves, you must admit that. He could have drawn a blue-print of her flat. Oh no!" He stopped dead. The others looked at him inquiringly. "You're not by any chance trying to tie him up with the burglary at Lady C's flat last night ? Are you telling us that was his game ?"

"I'm not telling you anything," said Oakapple, "because we haven't any proof. Simply that someone who knew she would be out last night took advantage of her absence. . . ."

"But she might have gone straight back from the meeting," Juliet began, and Rupert wound up soberly: "Only Paul would know she wasn't. And I've remembered something else. That night we had the demonstration outside the Embassy—there was a big burglary that evening. . . ."

"Paul was with us that night," said Ruth.

"But he knew Ambrose would be demonstrating. And he's a bachelor, and that coin collection of his was worth quite something. The police never recovered it, did they ?"

"Not yet," said Oakapple, smoothly.

"It's all speculation, isn't it ?" murmured Juliet, and her voice sounded none too steady. "It could be just coincidence."

"Had he been inside Mr. Ambrose's house ?"

"Had he ? Yes, I believe he had. He had the gift of the gab all right, and at first he went down very big. Only, of course, people get tired of hearing the same thing, and he didn't vary his speech much—we were agreeing that last night. . . ."

"And no one did this visiting before he joined your group ?"

"Well, I only came in shortly before he did," Ruth acknowledged, "but I certainly got the impression it was an innovation."

"Torquil supported it. He said an ounce of personal contact could be worth a ton of paper."

"Did this man ever give you the impression he was being threatened by anyone—quite outside your group's interests, that is ?"

"Why should he be ?"

"His landlady seemed to think he was getting letters."

"He never told us. But then he wasn't exactly an intimate type. Dead keen, though. Well, you have to be up pretty early in the morning to pull the wool over Torquil Holland's eyes."

"Does Torquil know about this ?" Juliet inquired.

"I haven't seen him yet. Will he be coming along this morning ?"

"He might, but he didn't say anything last night."

"He said a mouthful," ejaculated Rupert.

Oakapple asked them for a record of their meetings since Paul joined the strength, and Ruth took one from a file and handed it over. It seemed to Oakapple they were all more shocked on Torquil's account or the group's account than for the dead man. Indeed, once the first moment of incredulity had passed, they'd seemed to accept the fact of murder with quite remarkable equanimity. He asked them for an account of their individual movements the previous evening—a routine inquiry, he said—and none of them seemed hesitant or wary. Rupert said he and Colin Grant had gone along to Eve's flat. Eve was Evelyn Stone, the only one of the three who had a private flat, self-contained and everything—the rest had bed-sitters—and had played records there until some miserable old nanny-goat on the floor below had banged on the ceiling with a broomstick, after which they'd drifted off. That 'ud be round about midnight. Juliet had been washing her hair, Ruth had been at the flea-pit, no one knew about Torquil. He asked for Torquil's address.

" And I'd be obliged if none of you would telephone him to say I'm on my way," he added.

After he had gone they all agreed that sounded pretty ominous. Ruth, indeed, said defiantly it was a free country and if you wanted to telephone a pal—but Rupert stopped that at once.

" Do use your loaf, Ruthie. Even Julie can see that wouldn't work. The inspector would only have to ask Tork if anyone had rung up, and you know how he is when it comes to tampering with facts. He'd give himself away at once, and probably find himself being arrested on the spot. You know," he added, reflectively, " good lord, here's a bun-faced inquirer coming in, don't sell the pass, any of you. . . ." Over his shoulder he completed his sentence, " The police are a pack of unsophisticates at heart. They really do believe an innocent man has nothing to hide."

It was probably as well that Oakapple couldn't hear him. Like Queen Victoria, he would not have been amused.

CHAPTER V

19 ECCLESTON TERRACE was a tall, shabby, nondescript house. Torquil had a room at the back, characterless and barely-furnished. When he opened the door in response to the policeman's knock, Oakapple saw a battered suitcase half full of casually rolled clothes, and a rucksack, containing shoes and books, standing on a table. A camera in its case lay on the crowded bed. It was the one expensive thing in the room.

" Police ? " said Torquil. " Come in. You won't mind if I get on with my packing. Time presses."

If he was surprised at Oakapple's appearance he didn't show it.

"I dare say your friends told you I was on my way," the inspector said.

Torquil did look surprised then. "No, why? Should they?"

"I just thought—you're going away, Mr. Holland?"

"I'm joining a friend in the country to-night to get the gen for this job, and next week we fly to Africa."

Not a chap who did things by halves, Oakapple decided. "Is that a sudden plan?"

"In a way. That is, I intended to make the journey as soon as opportunity offered. I didn't realise it would come so suddenly."

"You haven't mentioned it to anyone?"

Torquil still seemed too much absorbed in what lay ahead—always living in the middle of next week, Rupert had said—to show any curiosity about this visit. He might have policemen calling every day of the week, like the milkman.

"I haven't had much chance," he replied, and smiled for the first time. "It wasn't till last night I realised my chance had come." Then the penny did seem to drop, and he inquired, "What is it? If you've seen any friends of mine—have you been to headquarters?"

A little surprised that he should dignify that one shabby room with such a title, Oakapple explained.

"We're inquiring into the death of a man known to you, I believe, as Paul Luzky."

Torquil, who had picked up a shoe and was wrapping it carelessly in a piece of newspaper, now let it fall to the ground.

"Death?"

"Yes. You haven't seen the paper this morning? Or heard the news on the radio?"

"I glanced at the headlines, but he'd scarcely make those."

"You might have noticed that a body had been found in a telephone kiosk in Brandon Passage."

"And that was Luzky—not that that's his real name, of course, but it's the one he used. Well, fancy my forgetting that one." Oakapple looked stunned; whatever reaction he'd anticipated it hadn't been this of mere surprise at his own forgetfulness, whatever that might mean; not even shocked by the news—but perhaps he'd been anticipating it. A cool customer and one to be watched.

" What was it you forgot ? " Oakapple inquired bluntly.

" That there was a phone box there. He'd said he had to telephone, and I proposed to stop him at any price. I tried Kidderminster Street and the three boxes by the station and one opposite the Dog and Pheasant, and I went up Barnes Road, there's one there by that phony little antique shop—but he wasn't in any of them. Queer I shouldn't have remembered there was a box in the passage." He thought for a moment, a deliberate kind of chap for all his tempestuous ways, and added, " Are you telling me he was murdered ? "

" Well, sir, it's hard to see how he could have hit himself on the back of the head with a brick."

" So he was cheating out on someone else, I suppose, who was a greater believer in direct action than we are. Do you know who did it ? He was all right at 10.30 last night."

Really, thought Oakapple, impatiently, how innocent can you be ? " I was hoping you might be able to help me. So far as my inquiries go you're the last person to have seen him alive. He might have said something. . . ."

" I can only tell you that I met him at the Casbah and told him we now knew he wasn't the chap he was pretending to be, and he didn't even put up a fight. He admitted he wasn't a Hungarian, had never been in that country. Why he played this elaborate joke (because I suppose it was a joke to him) I couldn't tell you, unless he'd had blackmail in mind from the start."

" Blackmail ? That's a serious charge, Mr. Holland."

" Look," expostulated Torquil, with a great show of reason, " I agree there's no necessity for calling a spade a bloody shovel, but it's sheer pomposity to describe it as an implement for the cultivation of the soil. A spade's a spade, and Luzky (so-called) was a crook. And he wasn't doing it for laughs. When I told him we'd rumbled him he said he was going to get in touch with some Fleet Street hound and spill the beans—tell them it was a put-up job between us, him and me. He said he could make quite a packet that way, seeing how many big names have been involved with the movement, though I dare say it seems small beer to you. On the other hand, if I cared to come to terms, his terms, he'd vanish without trace."

"And what were his terms ?"

"I didn't ask for details. I knew they'd be out of my reach, but if they hadn't been I wouldn't have paid him." And he quoted with an abrupt laugh, "Though you may pay them the Danegeld you do not get rid of the Dane."

"And so ?"

"He said I could have till midday to think over his proposal, meaning, I imagine, to raise whatever sum he had in mind. Then he left, saying he had some telephoning to do and he preferred not to do it from the pay phone in the Casbah. After he'd gone it occurred to me this was just another bit of double-crossing, he meant to have it both ways, my cheque for whatever I could raise, and the down payment for his articles. So I bolted after him, and, as I said, I was mad enough to forget about the box in the passage. I say, find a chair or something. I feel like the Day of Judgment with you looming over me like that."

But the room only contained two chairs, and both were filled to overflowing. Oakapple seated himself gingerly on the edge of the bed.

"And that's the last you saw of him ?"

"Yes."

"If you had found him what did you propose to do ?"

"Prevent him ringing his pals."

"Had you any particular plan in mind ?"

"First catch your hare. But I didn't propose to murder him. It's true the Brigade can do with all the publicity it can get, but not that kind—or Luzky's kind either, come to that."

"You feel very strongly about the Brigade, Mr. Holland?"

"Inspector," said Torquil, "I started this work nearly five years ago. I'd been visiting the camps in Europe, later I saw some of the Arab barbed-wire enclosures, I thought, this is called civilisation, and this is how men and women live, and where children are born. It was after I saw that that I understood how men can go to war. Till then I hadn't believed any sane man could not be a pacifist. I wanted to set society on fire, make people see the kind of world they lived in and enjoyed. A bigger slice of the cake, fair shares for all—it makes a bloody joke of everything we've been brought up to believe."

"And that's how it all started?"

"And you think it's pretty small beer? The first sign of animal life on this earth was a kind of moving jelly; you wouldn't have thought Shakespeare or Abraham Lincoln could spring from that. And all history's the story of one man—Livingstone in Africa—Napoleon in France—yes, Hitler in Germany, Lister in the world of medicine, all turning the world upside down. . . ."

"And Luzky was part of your ammunition?"

"Quite so."

"Mr. Holland, when you didn't find him last night—in a phone box, I mean—did you go back to the Casbah? I understand it stays open till about midnight."

Torquil looked at the shoe in his hand, wrapped it in another bit of paper and pushed it into the rucksack.

"No. Why should I? I mean, none of our lot was there so far as I could see, and if they had been I'd already blown my top in the Duck and Daisy. No, I decided to come back here."

"By train? Bus? Taxi . . .?"

"Taxi?" Torquil looked as startled as if he'd been asked if he rode home on his own private dragon. "Of course not, I walked. I'm a countryman," he added. "Walking's second nature to me."

"You walked alone?"

Torquil nodded. "I came back by the river, through Fulham Road and Kings Road, Chelsea, and through to Battersea Bridge."

"Not a very quick way to get back to Eccleston Terrace."

"I wasn't in any hurry. And I like walking by the river

at night, there aren't many people about. I walked through to Millbank—I remember passing the Tate and wondering why we don't keep our picture galleries open in the evening. That's when they'd be crowded. Chaps working all day would appreciate the chance—I wonder no one's suggested it to the Board of Education."

" Perhaps they have," said the inspector equably. " And then ? "

" I crossed the bridge by Lambeth Palace and walked to Westminster Bridge and thought of Wordsworth "—he seemed to be talking more or less to himself now, but the inspector let him run on—" and then I walked back down Victoria Street. It must have been soon after midnight when I got in. I have my own key, so I didn't need to disturb anyone."

" And when did you decide to leave town ? "

" Oh, that blew up with amazing suddenness, I thought at the time it's what's loosely called a dispensation of Providence. There's an expedition going out to Africa in connection with political prisoners, it's harder to work up sympathy for them than it is for refugees, everyone understands what it's like not to have a roof over your head, directly you mention politics personal prejudices start to operate. After I left the Duck and Daisy last night I rang this man, Jordan's the name, and said if any chance should surface, I was his man and he said, I've been trying to get *you*, one of our photographers has got himself involved in a car crash and we could include you in the expedition if you can raise the fare. Well, I just about could, and with this Luzky business coming up, nothing could have been better. I thought, I'll settle his hash—it didn't occur to me he'd brazen it out once he'd been uncovered, thankful if we didn't take him to court—and then I'll be off. I agreed to go down to-night, and I was going along to headquarters to tell Rupert Bowen—you've met him ? Yes, I can see you have—to carry on as usual when I'm out of the way. . . ." He brooded. " As a matter of fact, it was he who took up Luzky's credentials, and on the face of it they seemed imposing enough."

" And you really thought that this man would fade out at a word ? "

" I thought he'd be glad of the chance to get out without further trouble. You know, Inspector, he had all the gen at his fingertips, he must have known the real Luzky. . . ." And then he asked the question the inspector had been waiting for, " Does anyone know who he was ? "

" He has been identified," the inspector acknowledged, slowly. " Though we've had no confirmation as yet."

" Does it explain why he should think it worth his while? "

Oakapple said politely, " Your guess is as good as ours. I'm afraid you'll have to postpone your journey, Mr. Holland."

Even then the penny didn't drop. " You mean, to attend the inquest ? What can I tell you that Bowen or any of the crowd can't ? And anyway, the expedition doesn't start for five days. I shall be pretty busy—thank goodness, I had most of the essential injections last year, but . . ."

" You'll be notified about the time of the inquest," said Oakapple. " And, purely as a matter of routine, I'd like the name and address of the leader of the expedition. We have to have corroboration for every statement in a matter like this."

" Anyone would think you suspected I banged him on the head," observed Torquil, stormily. And then, " Oh no, that's absurd. I tell you, I never saw him again after he left the Casbah."

: : : :

" Old Torquil slays me," Rupert confided to Ruth not long after this conversation. " We all know he's got a heart of oak, but there are times when I think he's got a head to match."

For some time after the inspector, having put a few more questions and given no indication whether or no he believed the answers, had departed, Torquil stayed put, trying to weigh up the implications. Then he went to the slot-machine telephone on the landing and asked for a trunk call. But the operator told him the number was engaged.

At the Casbah the slim olive-skinned youth behind the counter agreed that someone had asked for Luzky the night before, a stranger speaking with a slightly foreign accent. He could give no detailed description of him, except that he was very well-dressed and looked a bit out of place in the coffee bar. So many people crowded in of an evening that individuals seldom made much impression, but he did recall Torquil. There had been an argument and a cup had been overturned and broken. He hadn't noticed the time.

When Oakapple returned to the station he learned that the matter had taken a dramatic turn. A tan gaberdine raincoat had been found stuffed under the seat in an Inner Circle train that had been shunted into a siding around midnight. The coat, which bore no signs of identification beyond the makers' trade mark, was heavily stained with blood. According to the records this train should have passed through Brandon Street Station at about 11.12, but the fog had slowed up all traffic, and it had been about fifteen minutes late. Oakapple arranged for a statement to this effect to appear in the Press, and sent a request to the B.B.C. to put out a note in the midday news, asking for any information to be given instantly to the police, telephone number supplied.

Tom Fenner, hurrying over the road to place a bet on the 2.30 at the newly-opened betting shop, heard the message and realised at once that now, Bess or no Bess, he couldn't keep his mouth shut any longer. For some reason, he expected the police to be grateful to him for his assistance (Arthur Crook could have told him better), but they simply wanted to know why he'd kept his trap shut so long. Or didn't he get up in time to read the morning papers?

"How was I to know he'd come out of the passage?" demanded Tom. "I'm not radar. And he said the marks were paint." No, he said later, he couldn't describe him, barring the facts that he was a tall chap and hatless. He'd vanished down the steps to the trains. So far as he could tell, there'd been no one else hanging about at the time. There had been a taxi standing outside the station, but a chap came out of the fog and hailed it. And no, he hadn't got its number. Who did they think he was? The electronic brain?

He put the time at 11.15 or thereabouts. He and his mates had been to the dogs and stopped at The Happy Goat for a pint *en route* for home. His bus went from Brandon Street Station; he'd seen the morning paper, but seeing he wouldn't know the chap again it hadn't seemed worth while—and he was on piece-work and they knew what that meant, didn't they? Voice? Well, it had sounded a bit queer. What did he mean by queer? Unnatural, the sort of voice husbands employ when wives ask awkward questions. He'd say the chap had had a skinful, but he hadn't fallen down the steps and he'd said the bit about red paint fast enough.

He supplied the police with his address reluctantly; by this time he didn't trust them any more than Crook did.

Information came seeping in. A cloak-room attendant from the Gents' toilet at Brandon Street Station had found a blood-stained towel in the disposal bin, and marks of blood on one of the wash-basins. And though the basin had been cleaned, the towel was available, and the blood found to tally with that staining the raincoat, and both were identical with the blood group of the dead man.

"Though there's nothing particularly significant about that," Oakapple agreed. "It would apply to about forty per cent of the people in this country. The description Fenner gives would fit Holland," he added, "and don't remind me it would also fit about forty thousand other people. Still, there can't have been so many hanging round the station in last night's fog, and he doesn't have an alibi."

"Point is, has he got a mackintosh and, if so, when did he acquire it? You might get after that, George. And—you've checked his yarn about the expedition?"

"That's confirmed by this fellow, Jordan. Seems to think the world of Holland. Got a good record, gave up a safe job to start on the refugee problem, does a bit of free-lancing—may have money of his own, but from what I've seen it wouldn't be his own for long. And I doubt if his earnings put more than a smear of butter on his bread, and thankful sometimes, I dare say, if there's even bread."

"Cuts both ways," said the superintendent gloomily. "A chap like that is going haywire if anyone—a little crook like Aslett say—threatens to wreck his set-up."

"He fixed with Jordan to join his crowd before he went to the Casbah," Oakapple reminded him.

"And before he realised that Aslett had him on the hop. These chaps with single-track minds give us more trouble than any of the pros. They're so apt to think of themselves as above the law. Better get the point about the raincoat settled first of all."

"And if he says he never had one?"

"We know he had one. Crook's prepared to swear to that, says he was carrying it when he came into the Duck and Daisy. And carrying it when he bounced out again. He can't give us any description except that it was the usual fawn-coloured affair and had a belt. He noticed it was dragging a bit."

"Trust Crook. Funny to think of him assisting the police."

"Like to take a bet, George? If and when we make an arrest, what's the odds Crook turns up on the other side? It 'ud split his fat face in two to find himself blazing away at us across the court-room floor."

:: ::

Torquil had got his connection to Maintree, where the man, Jordan, lived, at a second attempt.

"What sort of a jam are you in?" Jordan demanded.

"Just civil service red tape," Torquil assured him. "I can't come down till to-night, in case they want me again for anything, but I take it they won't hold the inquest on a Sunday, so I'll thumb a lift to-morrow, and leave a telephone number—it'll be all right, I've told them all I know, which isn't much."

When Oakapple turned up for the second time Torquil suggested cheerfully, "You've come to give me the All Clear? Good. I've been on to Jordan, and he told me you'd been putting him through it."

" We're making inquiries about a mackintosh, a Burberry, in fact, that's been found near the scene of the crime, with a view to establishing ownership." (Family crest—blue book surmounted by handcuffs, reflected Torquil, irreverently.) " I believe you have a Burberry, Mr. Holland. Perhaps you could let me see it."

They had moved from the staircase into Torquil's room that now had the naked look of all rooms about to be abandoned.

" That's odd," said Torquil, reflectively. " I haven't seen it this morning. I didn't need it when I went out, and I certainly had it last night."

He looked round vaguely, as if he expected the raincoat to fall through the ceiling.

" You haven't packed it ? "

" I shan't need a raincoat where I'm going." He threw open a wardrobe door to reveal half a dozen empty hangers swinging on their deserted rail.

" I must have left it in the Casbah," he decided. " I came out in such a hurry—unless, of course, I put it on the parapet of the bridge, I told you I stood there for some minutes. . . ."

" Surely," Oakapple protested, " you'd have noticed you weren't wearing it when you came out into last night's fog ? "

" In the heat I was in then I don't suppose I'd have noticed the weather if I'd been stark naked. Not that I ever notice it much," he added easily.

" What was it like ? "

" Nothing striking about it. I bought it at one of the Lost Property sales. Chaps must be damned well-off or damned careless to leave the stuff they do in trains and never reclaim it. This one had travelled around quite a lot, but so long as it kept out the rain, and the makers' name was a guarantee of that, I wasn't fussy about appearances. Oh, but—you were saying something about a mackintosh being found in the neighbourhood. I dare say that could be mine."

"It wasn't found in the Casbah, but in an Inner Circle train, stuffed under a seat."

"Well, that settles one point. I wasn't anywhere near a train last night. No, I expect I left it at the coffee bar . . ."

"You hadn't telephoned them ?"

Torquil looked surprised. "I hadn't actually noticed it was missing."

"So if we ring them now, and there's no trace of a raincoat . . ."

"That won't prove much," Torquil assured him. "They get a pretty tough crowd there, chaps who really don't appreciate the difference between *meum* and *tuum*. If, at the end of the evening, there was a raincoat looking for an owner I don't think it would have to look long."

"In short," Oakapple suggested, "you're telling us you don't expect it to be found there."

"That's about the size of it. But that won't prove I didn't leave it there. It's of no great value," he added casually. "When I get back, if the chaps out there don't make mincemeat of us, and you never can tell, I'll get myself another from the same source."

"I must ask you to accompany me to the station to inspect the coat we have."

Torquil shrugged ; his lively face was alight with impatience.

"More red tape ? But, see here, Inspector, even if I can identify it, you won't be much further on. Because I didn't put it there, and you aren't going to find it very easy to get anyone at the Casbah to notice one odd customer. Anyway, why don't you ring the Casbah—there's a free-for-all phone on the landing—and if they've got one the odds are that's mine. It'll save everyone time and trouble."

While Oakapple telephoned the coffee house, the police officer who had accompanied him appeared as mysteriously as if he'd materialised out of the air, and waited with Torquil. The latter moved across to the window. Spring was coming up slowly, with a reluctance for which she couldn't be blamed. In the sooty little garden square opposite the snowdrops were out in little magical clusters, and crocuses pushed their gold and purple spears through their green hoods.

" Did you ever hear that saffron comes from the purple flowers, not the gold ? " he asked suddenly, and the officer started.

" I can't say I have, sir." He sounded as impassive as the little stone girl in the centre of the grass plot opposite, for ever offering an empty dish to a questing dove.

" Trust Mother Nature to lead you up the garden," Torquil ran on. " The sparrows always go for the gold ones, you notice."

" I don't know much about gardening," offered the man, as stiff as ever.

" Still, don't quote me. It may just be a rumour. You know as well as I do it doesn't do to believe everything you're told."

He could hear Oakapple's voice from the landing below. " I see," he was saying. " If you should get any information . . . Yes, thank you."

" No soap ? " suggested Torquil, when the inspector reappeared. " Don't say I didn't warn you."

" You're sure there's nothing special about your raincoat ? " Oakapple said, as they went down the stairs together.

" One of the buttons is an odd one," Torquil recalled. " I lost one in a bit of a shindy we had with some Fascists a while ago, and I replaced it with a black one. So if this coat doesn't have a black button—*ergo*, it's not mine."

And, of course, it hadn't got a black button. For the first time, Torquil showed some sense of shrinking when he was asked to examine the coat found in the underground train.

" Is that his blood ? Paul's, I mean ? "

" It could be."

They also took him along to see the dead man. " That's the chap. Well, he overplayed his hand at the last, didn't he ? " And he added, " Of course, if he was double-crossing us he could quite well have been double-crossing someone else, so all you've got to find out is who."

The Press that night reported that it was understood the police had uncovered some fresh clues in the telephone box murder ; a man had been at the station for part of the day assisting them in their inquiries ; it was believed an early arrest would be made.

CHAPTER VI

" I SAY, CONNIE, OLD THING, you remember that wog you were on about night before last ? "

Lord Charles was reading the Sunday paper. Between them he and Connie had five, four for news and one for the crossword.

" You shouldn't call people wogs, Charles." Connie was doing something to a vase of magnificent early roses in a corner of the drawing-room. " And he was charming. You ought to have stayed to meet him." Already her recollection of the evening was slightly vague, and she forgot that it was the " wog " who had departed of his own accord.

" Well, it's too late now," declared Lord Charles in the same buoyant voice. " Chap's dead. Found his body in a telephone box. Funny thing," brooded Lord Charles. " Same shape as a coffin, really."

" Of course it isn't," retorted Connie. " They have to have a wide bit for the folded arms. And I don't know what you're talking about. That man in the telephone box was killed on Friday."

" That's what I said. Your wog."

" If you mean Mr. Heinz, he was alive on Saturday because he sent these roses, and it's the first time I've heard of a ghost buying flowers."

" You've got it wrong. Not that one. Your little black bear."

" Oh ! " Connie momentarily lost interest in the roses. " Do they know who did it ? "

" Oh, lord, yes. They've been grilling a chap down at

the station ever since yesterday. 'An early arrest is anticipated,'" he quoted from the *Sunday Rag*.

"So that's why he didn't come back. Charles, is Muffy Urquhart in town?"

"How on earth should I know? He's presiding at this Borden trial to-morrow. . . ."

"Well, you might try and get in touch. He's known to be very sympathetic with foreigners. And that's what Franz Heinz is, if he has got American nationality now."

"I hope you know what you're talking about," said Charles. "Because I don't."

"It's perfectly obvious the man they're grilling is poor Franz. I don't suppose he knows what his rights are—they do things differently in America. . . ."

"He'll be warned before he's questioned, and he can have a lawyer. . . ."

"He won't know a lawyer, not over here. Ring Muffy and ask him who's the best man to get, and get him before the prosecution has a chance."

"Connie, I know you've always been half-way up the wall," her husband protested. "Now you seem to be skating along the top of it. (*a*) We don't know this chap they've got is your wog at all. (*b*) Even if he is, he hasn't been arrested yet, and he may simply be helping them to put a case together against someone else."

"How can he?" demanded Connie, scornfully. "He doesn't know anyone here, how can he try and pass the baby on?"

"And (*c*)," Charles continued, patiently, "if he does find himself in a jam he's got a perfectly good Embassy to protect his interests. The American Embassy in Eisenhowerplatz," he elaborated in the patient voice of a man who believes he is talking in words of one syllable. "Don't tell me you've never seen that shocking great eagle towering over the square. It's my belief that if Hitler could have seen that he'd have called the war off before he did, and don't remind me it wasn't there in Hitler's day."

"Don't forget to ring Muffy," called Lady Connie from the hall. She had conjured up a minute hat and a fur coat from nowhere, it seemed, and already she was at the front door. " Anyway, the Americans are our allies. It's up to us. . . ." The door slammed. Lord Charles groaned and mixed himself a whisky-and-soda. Oh well, he reflected, the police had just had a rise in pay, no sense blaming Connie for seeing that they earned it.

They knew Connie quite well at the local nick. " It's not the car this time," she told them, before anyone could ask what she wanted. She could never understand why the authorities were so unsympathetic about her little bubble-car. " I've never run over anything worse than a piece of paper," she would protest.

The station sergeant supposed she'd come down to inquire how they were getting on in the search for her jewellery, but she waved that aside with an elegant white-gloved hand.

" I'd forgotten about that. I'm sure you're doing all you can. No, it's Mr. Heinz . . ." She ran on like Tennyson's Brook for a while, and no one tried to stop her. If you gave her her head and listened intently you generally found yourself in possession of all the salient facts by the time the fountain of her speech had run dry. Then they assured her they didn't know anything about a Mr. Heinz.

" Oh well, in that case," beamed Connie, " let's forget all about it. I must get back and warn Charles not to ring up the judge—Judge Urquhart, that is—I was thinking, the stranger within the gate . . ."

" Just a minute, if you please. You say this Mr. Heinz went to meet the deceased on Friday night ? "

" Ah, but I don't think he could have met him, because he was going to bring him back to the Savoy, and he didn't. Or perhaps he changed his mind. You know what foreigners are, so much more emotional than the British."

Authority indicated as nicely as it could that even foreigners, with American passports, can't be allowed to go round London being emotional with half-bricks. They wanted to know more about the mysterious Mr. Heinz.

" Simply divine," Connie assured them. " My grandmother . . ."

Charles would have known what she was driving at, but the police were utterly at sea.

"Your grandmother wasn't one of the party at the Savoy?" asked the officer, politely, but mystified, too.

"Wherever she may be now I'm sure she wishes she had been," Connie told him.

"Have you Mr. Heinz's address? His hotel, I mean?"

"Be sure you tell him of his rights before you start asking questions," said Connie earnestly. "And if he doesn't seem upset at the news, don't be surprised, because I got the impression he didn't really like this Paul Luzky. He said he was dead. That's why he left us, he went to make sure."

When they had sorted out her statement they let her go back to Charles, quivering with indignation on Heinz's behalf, and a man went round to the chap's hotel. Heinz was a great deal calmer than Lady Connie had been. He agreed he had gone to the Casbah, but the man he saw there, who was passing himself off as Paul Luzky, was an impostor. He, Heinz, had heard some two years earlier of the real Luzky's death; why anyone should want to use his name was no concern of his (Heinz's). He repeated what Paul had told him, and said that he had left the Casbah at about 10.30. There was a watchmaker next door, with an immense clock over the entrance and he'd checked his own timepiece.

"You didn't go back to the Savoy?"

"I was no longer in the mood for drinking champagne."

"You came straight back to your hotel?"

"That was my intention, but it was foggy, there were no cabs to be had, I had recourse to the underground. . . ."

"Which station would that be?"

He shrugged. "I do not recall. This is my first visit to London. At all events the train did not take me to my destination. I should have changed, they said . . ."

"It's all perfectly probable," Oakapple agreed with Superintendent Barnet. "He wouldn't be likely to get a cab at that hour of the night—wait a minute, didn't Fenner say something about a chap coming out of a side-street and hailing a taxi?"

"But this chap says he didn't get a taxi. He came by underground. Probably whizzing up and down stairs at the various stations like a yo-yo. Anyway, if the dead man isn't Luzky, what motive did he have?"

"We don't know, do we? The real Luzky may have mentioned his name to the fake one."

"But the fake one couldn't do anything about it unless he was going to make a clean breast of his own deception, and that 'ud put him in Queer Street. For one thing, he'd been getting money by false pretences, and I don't think the law says anywhere it makes a difference if you get the money for a good cause."

"He could have known something that wouldn't do Heinz any good if it came out."

"With the real article dead, what proof would he have?"

"The dear B.P. doesn't worry its head much about proof. And you know as well as I do how mud sticks."

"It rather depends who chucks it. This chap was a self-confessed fraud. . . ."

"Did you ask Heinz about the Burberry?"

"He swears he never owned one. He's got a sort of light raincoat, but he was wearing a black topcoat that night. Lady Connie confirms that, and the lad at the Casbah says he noticed he was particularly well turned-out, probably stuck out in that crowd like a sore thumb—though he won't swear to the colour of the coat the chap had on."

The valet at The Chesterfield, that august hotel much-loved for some reason by American tourists, probably because in their view it dates back to the days of Dickens and some express surprise that it's even got electricity, said he had never seen a Burberry among Mr. Heinz's wardrobe. Guests' clothes were automatically collected and brushed, and sponged where necessary, every day. No trace of blood had been found on anything he wore; the shoeblack said there hadn't been any traces on the soles of his shoes, either.

Heinz, told he would be required for the inquest, dug in his toes.

"What conceivable assistance can I give you?" he

demanded. "A man I never saw before, and whose name I do not know."

"At least you know who he wasn't, and that could be important." But Oakapple frowned as he said it. All the evidence to date seemed negative. The dead man, according to Crook, was one Jack Aslett, but no one had been found to confirm this. He appeared to have no relations, no sweetheart, not even any friends. The Peace Brigade couldn't help much. None of them could recall him saying anything that would be of help now, but then they had only known him as Luzky, so that wasn't very surprising. The landlady did not recall his ever having a visitor or any personal telephone call. There had been a few letters, but she could give no details. She repeated her story of secret threats, without producing any corroborative evidence. The police were like the dolt in the middle of the room in a game of Puss In The Corner. No matter how agile they were or how conscientious, every corner they tried to bound into was occupied. The search for Walter Smith, who had identified the body taken from the river as that of Jack Aslett proved abortive. The address he had given two years before proved to be part of an area destined for inclusion in a new schools programme; some of the occupants of the demolished houses had asked the Town Hall for assistance in finding alternative accommodation, but Walter Smith wasn't among them. All over the country men called Walter Smith were being irritated by strangers, in or out of uniform, calling at their houses and asking questions. [The *Sunday Rag* went to town on the story the following week.] The police, realising that Heinz answered Fenner's description quite as adequately as Torquil Holland —neither man had worn a hat and they were of similar height and build—arranged an identity parade at which both men were ordered to attend. This was held forty-eight hours before Torquil was due to leave with his expedition. The police called at Tom Fenner's home to make sure he attended. "I wonder you don't bring your beds with you," Bess Fenner snapped. "Tom's a working man—and working men ought to be paid overtime."

Fenner walked along the row of men assembled for his scrutiny; he asked if he could hear them speak. That knocked out four with cockney accents, and it also knocked out Heinz. "This chap wasn't a foreigner. I know he talked a bit queer, but it was lah-di-dah queer."

Eventually he said he couldn't put the finger on any of them. There'd been a fog, the encounter had only lasted a few seconds, he couldn't even tell you if the fellow had been light or dark.

"Mind you, he had hair," he said.

"I thought he stepped into the light when he went into the station."

"Cor stone the crows," expostulated Fenner. "I wasn't looking any higher than the top button of his coat by that time, and if it had been you, mate, you'd have been the same."

"Well, that lets Heinz out. We can't detain an American citizen on such information as we've got," opined Barnet, gloomily. "Holland's another matter."

In spite of stringent inquiries no trace had turned up of a raincoat with one black button that might have been identified with the one Torquil had lost. A notice had been put up in the Casbah asking if anyone had inadvertently removed a raincoat not his own property, in which case he was asked to return it. Inquiries had also been made in case he had left it on the parapet of the bridge as he had himself suggested; and telephone kiosks were searched, since he recalled ringing up his friend, Jordan, before he went along to the Casbah. But the result was always the same.

"It doesn't mean the coat still doesn't exist somewhere," Oakapple admitted, falling over backwards in his effort to be fair to a suspected man. "It could have been lifted by someone who doesn't want to draw attention to himself, or by someone who doesn't read the papers, or possibly can't read, some of these old layabouts you find on the Embankment or sleeping in the parks are illiterate to the pitch of not even knowing the alphabet. It could have been pawned for a bob or two. . . ." But no pawnbroker would agree that he had set eyes on it. The members of the Peace Brigade had been questioned as to any particularity that might single this coat out, but no one spoke of a black-coloured button. Mrs. Tait, Torquil's landlady, was also interviewed by the police. She seemed to think they were here in connection with her boy, Dicky, who had had frequent brushes with authority. When they spoke of Torquil, she threw back her head and said she couldn't ask for a better lodger.

"Isn't it a fact he has a raincoat with one black button on it?" she was pressed.

"Suppose he has, is that any affair of yours?"

She had a nice independent manner with the police that Crook would have approved.

"If it wasn't do you suppose we'd be here? Now, come, Mrs. Tait, we're asking you a simple question. Did Mr. Holland have a raincoat with one button that didn't match the rest?"

"I couldn't say. Not that I ever noticed."

"You're sure you never sewed one on for him?"

"I never. Not that I wouldn't, but he never asked."

"But he did perhaps ask for a button and you couldn't find one the right colour?"

"I told you, I don't know anything about a black button. If he says there wasn't one, then there wasn't."

"Suppose he says there was?"

"I still wouldn't know."

"Would Dicky know?"

"Why can't you leave the boy alone?"

"Is he around anywhere?"

"I don't know where he is and that's the truth. He's got his own life to live, hasn't he?"

It was like that at every turn. Every time a blood-orange or a good cigar, Crook used to chant. But all these oranges had gone rotten on them and the cigars were mouldy. They started inquiries from the other end, looking for someone outside the Peace Brigade who might be glad to see Aslett under the sod. Although they didn't disbelieve Crook when he said the chap was a wrong 'un, still they hadn't got his fingerprints at the Yard. And though they combed through their records nothing and no one tied up with a man answering his description, acting as partner or stool-pigeon or go-between or what-have-you with any of the acknowledged gangs. But an uncomfortable number of households where the dead man had visited in connection with the Peace Brigade had subsequently been robbed, though not always on the night when the owner was speaking for what the *Daily Screech* called The Cause. Police took a picture of Paul round all the pubs where small-time con. men and thieves were known to foregather, but no one would put a name to him. If he was known to the fences they weren't talking, and though the authorities let it be known they were prepared to pay for information, no demands were made on their exchequer. So—since there was no evidence of trouble between him and his partners (since they couldn't even identify his partners), they were driven back to their original field of inquiry. A man came forward to say he'd overheard Torquil remark that, if he thought there was a possibility of Paul carrying out his threat, he'd kill him himself.

"Those were his words. If you harm this work we're doing, I swear it, I'll kill you. Quite quiet. It was frightening really."

And so, on the day after Franz Heinz returned to the States, a free man, a warrant was issued for the arrest of Torquil Holland on a charge of murder.

CHAPTER VII

"BILL," SAID MR. CROOK just after the news broke, "I'm expecting to hear from those Peace Brigadiers any day now. And I'll be ready and waiting. I've got all the gen from the police and the Press and one or two ideas of my own to top up with."

"Any special reason why they should come here?" murmured Bill.

" Well, I gave them my card that night in the pub. And what was the sense of me going to the Duck and Daisy at all, not my cup o' tea by a long chalk, if it wasn't *meant* ?" inquired the simple-minded Mr. Crook. " No, they'll be along, you'll see."

Twenty-four hours later they surfaced. Three of them came like a deputation, Rupert and the two girls. He supposed the young man headed the party because he was Torquil's stand-in, and each girl felt she could add something to the story, and it wouldn't bother them, not if he knew women, if those somethings clashed like cymbals. He was rather partial to cymbals himself.

They brought into that office, where so many shady, broken, sly and desperate characters had come, an air of such youth and credulity it seemed to paint the uninteresting tea-coloured walls with a brighter hue. He saw, and was oddly moved by the sight, that it occurred to none of them that he would let Torquil be convicted.

He opened the ball by asking if Torquil knew they'd come.

" I saw the old boy yesterday," confirmed Rupert. " I didn't for one moment suppose his precious family would ante up—they cut him out of their respective wills years ago, a blasted reactionary that's how they think of him, but if their blood's thicker than water the water must be practically invisible."

" How is he ? " asked Crook.

" Sometimes I think he's the most conceited chap I know," Rupert replied, and even Mr. Crook was a bit shaken out of his normal composure. " Yes, honestly, Julie. If it was me in his shoes I'd be sweating in every pore, wondering how I was going to get out of the jam, but not old Torquil. Dear me, no. If an angel walked through the prison wall and handed him a free pardon he wouldn't even be surprised It's what he expects."

" That's the best way to get one," Crook told them. " Now, remember, anything you say here goes no farther than these walls unless we can twist it into something useful.

You all know the chap, I've only seen him once. Is there the remotest chance he might have done it ?"

"What on earth do you expect us to say to that ?" Rupert demanded. "If we say there was one chance in a hundred you won't touch the case."

"I was fighting in France when your grannie was wondering which kind the stork was going to bring her," Crook pointed out. "So don't start telling me what I'd do. A plain yes or no is all I'm asking."

"Well, then," said Rupert, "the answer's obviously no."

He brought out the words with a vigorous defiance that was in itself an admission of doubt.

Ruth had no such reservations. "Of course, he didn't do it," she said impatiently. "You've seen him, Mr. Crook. Torquil . . ."

"I never heard such a name," Crook burst forth. "Why didn't they christen him Samson and be done with it ? Honest, I thought he was going to uproot the pillars and bring the roof down round our ears, and I dare say he would have done if there'd been any pillars to uproot." He looked at Julie. "What say you ? Guilty or Not Guilty ?"

"I don't say he wouldn't be capable of throttling someone who cheated out on him, but if he did he wouldn't run away afterwards."

"Stay and justify himself ? You could be right, sugar. Anyway, this wasn't throttling, this was a brick."

"So, of course, I say Not Guilty, too."

"Well, that clears the air. Now, I've seen all the statements made to the police, including your own. Anything anyone wants to add? F'r instance," he looked at Ruth. "I see where you told the rozzers you'd seen dear Paul talking to a stranger. D'you remember if he wore a raincoat ?"

"He didn't," said Ruth at once. "He wore a black coat, probably the first they'd ever seen at the Casbah. He looked thoroughly out of place, like one of those spy films."

"And he says he was wearing a black coat, and the valet says there wasn't any Burberry in his luggage, so that seems to frank him. We know my client was carrying his coat when he left the Duck and Daisy; according to him he rang up this pal of his from a call-box in Dedham Street, but there's no trace of a coat there now, though that ain't proof he didn't leave it there. . . ."

"No," said Ruth. "He was wearing it at the Casbah that night."

"Who says so?" exclaimed Crook, sharply. "There's nothing in the reports I've seen to indicate that anyone saw him after he left the Duck and Daisy."

Ruth looked defiant. "The police didn't ask me, and anyway I couldn't help them. But I passed the Casbah and saw Paul talking to this man. I'd meant to drop in and ask if Julie had given him the gipsy's warning, but I couldn't interrupt. He was someone I'd never seen before. And then I saw Torquil arrive, wearing the coat, and I guessed it would be too late anyway. So I went on to my flea-pit, hardly worth it, they close at 10.45, but you know how it is. . . ."

"He probably left it in the Casbah," urged Julie. "If you'd ever been inside that place in the evening, you'd know nothing short of a grizzly bear could endure a coat for more than five seconds."

"Then it'll be there now, won't it?"

They all looked dubious. "It's a bit of a free-for-all," Rupert acknowledged.

"And how about Mr. Heinz?" Crook pressed on. "He seems to have stuck to his coat by all accounts."

"Oh well, he's an American. They have central heating there."

He saw they all considered that a perfectly adequate answer.

"Anyway, Torquil must have been born with an extra skin or something," contributed Rupert. "He never seemed to notice the weather. Well, you saw for yourself he wasn't even wearing the coat at the Duck and Daisy."

"Would any of you recognise it if you saw it?"

"You mean, could the one the police found actually be his?"

" I mean, could any of you say definitely if it was his or not ? "

Rupert looked dubious. " Well, you know the way of it, Mr. Crook. All these coats look very much alike. I once took Col's instead of my own and I wore it for a week before I discovered my mistake, and then only because of something I found in the pocket. Poor old Col ! Were his ears red ? "

" Point taken," said Crook, smoothly. " Now *you*," this time he addressed himself to Julie, " saw Paul at the Casbah, you spoke to him. Did he give you the impression he was expecting anyone ? "

" No. But he didn't make any move to go when I warned him Torquil was thirsting for his blood."

" Remember anything he said ? "

" Yes, because it struck me as rather odd. He said, ' You tell Torquil one of these days he'll find he's bitten off more than he can chew. And how surprised he's going to be when he finds himself choking to death.' "

" Didn't offer any explanation ? No ? So he wasn't afraid of what your pal might offer to do to him. And we know, from what Torquil (he seemed to curl his tongue round the unfamiliar name as if he couldn't quite encompass it) has said, that he believed he had the fifth ace up his sleeve. Now, I gather you, Bowen, had had suspicions already about Paul's bona fides. Not spoken of them to anyone ? "

Rupert shook his head. " I thought one day he'd put his foot right in it, and then we could get shot of him, but in the meantime he had his uses. As a matter of fact, it's being pretty tough trying to keep the office going since he passed in his checks."

" Much interest ? " inquired Crook kindly.

" Oh, the supply of ghouls is the one commodity that never runs short. They're even prepared to put a bob in the box in the hopes of learning some new development before it appears in the Press."

" Hadn't thought of putting up a Gone Away board till the hoo-ha dies down ? "

"Well, of course not," declaimed both girls vigorously. "It would look as if we hadn't any faith in Torquil. This is his baby. Because he can't look after it himself for the time being it doesn't mean it must be allowed to die. You don't kill five years' work so easily."

Crook's thought, which remained unexpressed, was that the man was bigger than the movement, in fact, that the man was the movement, and it was less a case of its abandoning him than of his forsaking it. Since this all appeared to him irrelevant he asked, "Now we've had this turn-out, any of you been asking yourselves why Paul was tied up with you at all?"

"He was using us as a cover, of course."

"Of course," Crook agreed. "And that's the angle from which we'll tackle it. The police have worked from the Peace Brigade point of view, we'll start from the opposite corner. Because if my client's innocent, as he has to be to qualify, then the enemy ain't in the Brigade, not as such, that is, but is concerned with the Hyde half of Paul's existence. Paul, the collaborator, the member of a gang who're interested in other people's possessions."

"Yes," Ruth acknowledged, "we did discuss that. I suppose he had to have a partner, he couldn't have been working on his own?"

"Ever tried selling hot stuff?" Crook murmured. "You need to be an expert, you have to know the markets, and you do need a cover man. He could simply have passed the stuff on to a fence and taken whatever the fellow offered, fifteen, twenty per cent. Or he could have had a partner and gone fifty-fifty. From our point of view that's the better solution, because it gives us someone to identify."

"The man in the blood-stained overcoat," said Rupert, promptly. "He went to meet Paul. . . ."

"By appointment," chimed in Ruth. "Mr. Crook, do you think it could have happened that way?"

"Well—but I thought Paul said he'd be waiting in the Casbah for your chum any time he arrived."

"I was thinking about that telephone call he made. Julie said he was phoning when she arrived."

" Making a date ? But he didn't know then that he'd been rumbled, and surely he wouldn't have left it till the eleventh hour. . . ."

" He could have been telling X that he'd got the stuff all right. . . ."

" No," said Rupert. Crook lay back and let them talk. Never do a job anyone will do for you, was one of his mottoes. " For one thing, we haven't any proof, have we, Mr. Crook, that he was involved with the Hunter burglary at all ? "

" Well, no," Crook acknowledged, " but some evidence is very circumstantial, like when you find a trout in the milk. Quotation," he added, hurriedly.

" And surely he'd have handed the stuff over before coming to the Casbah," Julie urged. " Obviously he hadn't got it then. . . ."

" Who says he hadn't ? He was wearing some sort of a coat, wasn't he ? And the missing stuff wasn't all that bulky—no tiara, f'r instance, just a necklace and some brooches and a few rather nice rings. Lady Connie had a simple soul, the best was always good enough for her. They'd go into a pocket. . . . What is it, sugar ? Tell your Uncle Arthur." For a new expression on Ruth's face brought him to a sudden halt.

" Why on earth did none of us think of it ? " she was marvelling. " We must all have been crazy. Mr. Crook, when the police found the body they didn't find any means of identification on it, did they ? "

" Too true," said Crook, " though, mind you, that ain't unusual. Think of the Found Dead and Found Drowned corpses that have to be advertised and can't always be identified even then, if no one comes forward. Think, if you like, of that body they took out of the river that was identified as Jack Aslett. If any of you was to be knocked down by a car on the way home could you be identified by the chap who picked you up ? "

Julie opened a bag, there was a letter in it. " Franks you," admitted Crook. " How about the others ? "

" I have a driving licence," Ruth pointed out, laying it on the table.

" I'll have to buy that one," Rupert acknowledged. " I don't run a car, and I'm not like a woman who carries one of these shopping cards in her bag. You know, the kind you get from Harrods or one of those Kensington stores."

" You haven't got my point," insisted Ruth, and now her voice sounded excited. " They said they found a wallet . . ."

" They say money talks," Crook agreed, " but it don't always say what you want it to."

" But—no one said anything about a brief-case."

That brought Crook up erect as a man steeling himself for the fatal shot to qualify for a hero's death.

" Are you telling me this character went around with a brief-case ? Did he have it that night ? "

" He always had it. We used to laugh at him. We'd say that if we were in a gaggle and a stranger was told one of us was a refugee, the last one he'd guess would be Paul. He wouldn't have been seen in our sort of get-up." (Crook, who wasn't precisely a fussy dresser himself, felt he couldn't blame him.) " The perfect civil servant, striped pants, unnoticeable dark coat, square-toed shoes, brief-case. The only thing he didn't cotton to was an umbrella. We decided it must be a party symbol behind the Iron Curtain, and he wasn't looking for trouble."

' Now—think before you answer—did he have this brief-case that night ? "

Three voices assured Crook at once that he had. " He kept his notes in it. Not that he ever looked at them. He must have known his speech by heart. Why, most of us could have done it for him, we'd heard it so often. But he carried it for effect."

Crook turned to Julie. " Now, sugar, it all depends on you. Did he have that case with him when you popped in to give him the green light ? "

" Yes," said Julie, with no hesitation at all. " I nearly fell over it."

" I wonder if my client noticed it. I'll tell you who didn't, and that's Tom Fenner, the chap who saw the man in the Burberry. Or if he did it didn't register with him.

Anyway, it 'ud be too easy if he was carrying a case, because a chap out on the booze, as he seems to have been, don't usually take a brief-case with him."

"If he's not concerned with the murder, why hasn't he come forward? Wouldn't that be the act of an innocent man?"

"It might seem so to you, but innocence is like justice, it don't only have to exist, it has to be shown to exist. As for not coming forward, he could have his own reasons."

"But Torquil's liberty is at stake," Julie cried.

"Maybe this chap's in the same boat. All prison warders don't wear H.M. uniform. And I've met chaps who'd find Dartmoor quite a nice change from life imprisonment with an ever-loving."

"But the blood!"

"I could cut my hand—I bleed like a pig anyway—and I could spoil that sassy suit you're wearing, but it wouldn't prove I'd come for you with a flick knife. Say he went to phone, fell over the body, got the fright of his life, he'd had a skinful according to Fenner, and his one idea was to get himself out of trouble. He must have had something to hide or he'd have got Fenner to come along and make certain he wasn't seeing things."

"Suppose Fenner declares he wasn't carrying a brief-case, who does that leave?"

"You're forgetting Walter, ain't you?" said Crook, looking genuinely surprised.

"Walter?"

"The chap who identified a body as that of Jack Aslett when we now know that Jack Aslett was alive and kicking up to, say, two weeks ago."

"He could have been mistaken, I suppose."

"Could he? With a missing finger-joint and a noticeable kind of ring—I've checked up on the inquest, and this fellow, Walter Smith, made a point of recognising the remains by means of the joint and the ring. And the gold tooth. The police have uncovered the chap who attended to Aslett's bridgework and there's no record of any gold tooth, supplied by him or by anyone else."

" Where do you start looking for him—Walter Smith, I mean ? "

" That's what you're paying me for, it's my headache," Crook assured them, sunnily. " That the police couldn't find him don't mean a thing. He doesn't have to be calling himself Walter Smith any more, he could change his appearance, change his address, you could be sitting next to him in the Tube. He's not one of the big operators, or they'd have tracked him down, but then Aslett wasn't a big operator either. About so high." He put out an immense leg-of-mutton hand at a distance about four feet above ground level. " That's why he worked on a small scale."

" Which is why he chose us as an umbrella, so to speak ? " suggested Rupert gloomily.

"Oh, he was no fool. Don't suppose it was just chance that brought him behind the bar of the Duck and Daisy. You'd been using the pub for quite a while, I gather."

" It was convenient for St. Katharine's Hall. We used that a lot. For one thing it made a sort of focus, enthusiasts used to follow us round, and they got to know where to look for us. And then that's a part of London with a big drifting population, lots of furnished rooms and hotels, people coming and going."

" So you could count on a fair number of waifs and strays," agreed Crook, in his outspoken way.

" And, if course, it was cheaper to hire than a hall in the West End. Torquil was always keen on keeping expenses down. He said one of the scandals of the age was the percentage of moneys received that went into overheads. He'd have talked at street corners if the police weren't so bloody-minded."

" There's always Hyde Park," Crook reminded him.

" Oh, he talked there all right. But you don't pick people up in the same way. We found the Duck and Daisy quite a useful place—chaps used to drift in and it's the kind of pub where women come along in pairs. . . ."

Crook suppressed a groan. That alone would have put the bolt on the door for him. The Two Chairmen was as exclusive as the Athenæum.

" And then Jim was very decent about it. I think in his heart he sympathised with us. A lot of landlords don't like it if you start passing round literature—of course, being a Free House made it easier for him."

" And I dare say Paul knew all that. I've seen a copy of your records, and they're quite impressive," acknowledged Crook, handsomely. " And once Paul had got himself installed behind the bar, it was a cinch he could latch on to you. And quite soon he's visiting the houses of the great, getting a dekko at the layout, deciding what's worth trying and what's out of reach."

" How would he know that Lady Connie, for instance, had fifteen thousand pounds worth of stuff on the premises?" Rupert asked.

" He's in the trade," explained Crook, patiently. " And knowledge is the one stock you can't afford to run short of. I asked Bill—that's the chap who let you in—notice him ?"

They nodded. Arthur Crook grinned. " He wasn't always on the side of the angels, Crook's angels, I mean, and it's been very helpful to me to have a chap who's been, so to speak, both sides of the curtain. He estimated the value of Lady C's jewels within fifty smackers—and he's been out of the game for more than twenty-five years. But he could still tell you which houses are worth chancing your arm—that is, seven years in quod—for, and what to look for when you do get in."

" And, of course, Paul knew Lady C. would be going on to the Savoy and wouldn't be back till all hours, he got her to show him all round the flat. . . ."

" And there was a party in the flat above, so a stranger wouldn't attract any attention. Of course, that was the wicked flourishing like a green bay tree, he can hardly have counted on that. Mind you," he added seriously, " don't imagine he's been timing these raids to coincide with your precious meetings. The police would have tumbled to his little game long ago if that had been the case. But he was able to map out a course—he didn't have to do all the jobs himself. Walter might have taken turns. Or, of course, Walter may only be the go-between. Too early yet to say."

" And why would Walter or anyone else want to bash his head in with a brick ? It doesn't make sense to me. Even if he was going to break with us. . . ."

" Operative word bein' break. And in fact it was like bein' broken. I'd say this was an unpremeditated murder until the last minute. I mean, you can't accidentally slug a chap with a brick. The way I see it is he gets in touch with X and they make the appointment at the phone box. As good a place as any to hand over the stuff, especially on such a night. He arrives first and goes in to give the impression he's going to make a call."

" Perhaps he actually did make a call."

Crook shook his head. " I asked the rozzers about that. He hadn't got a connection, and no coppers came back when they pressed Button B. What's more, he hadn't got four coppers in his loose change, so he never meant to make a call. Mind you, he might have been enticed there to take one. Be at the box in Brandon Passage at 11 p.m. and I'll ring that number. Not likely to be many people hanging around in that weather."

" I once took a call from a phone box," agreed Juliet, thoughtfully. " A strange voice said, ' Is that you, darling ?' and I said, ' Wrong number ' and hung up."

" You have to remember that Paul made that first call, the one from the Casbah, before he knew the balloon had gone up. X comes along and Paul tells him. We're finished, kaput, so far as the Brigade's concerned. We'll have to think of something else. And so they do, only they don't think along the same lines. X realises that your pal isn't going to let the case go by default, and the one thing he can't stand is publicity. Never be fooled by that yap about honour among thieves. Once Paul had been unfrocked, as it were, he stopped being an asset and became a positive danger. There was always the chance he'd turn Queen's Evidence, which featherbeds a chap, and there was nothing of the heroic mould about him. I met him once about three years ago—did I tell you ? The only hide he was interested in was his own. In a sense you could say X hadn't much choice. And he must have known he'd never have such a good chance again. Hist, someone's coming, take up that receiver—you can hear him, can't you ? And Paul, poor little runt, does as he's bid and wham ! I don't suppose he ever knew what hit him. What really riles me," he added, " is to think I walked past the box—X must have been a tallish chap to be able to smash that electric light bulb—with the murderer and his victim *in situ* and no little inner voice whispered, ' This is it.' Maybe I should apply for a hearing aid, after all."

" I should think it was a good thing your voice didn't whisper," said Ruth simply. " If you'd come upon X *in flagrante delicto* you mightn't be here now to get Torquil out."

Mr. Crook seemed genuinely surprised. " How come ? There were plenty more bricks lying around, and I pack a pretty healthy wallop myself."

" I bet you do," murmured Rupert respectfully. " Somehow one doesn't think of murder being as casual as that."

" Murder's never really casual," Crook assured him. " It starts in the mind long before it comes to fruition. It begins on the day you find yourself thinking, ' When Aunt Mary dies I shall inherit a fortune,' instead of ' If Aunt Mary died '—see ? "

" I still don't understand why they think they've got a sound case against Torquil," Juliet objected, and Crook said : " The policeman's sacred Trinity, means, motive and opportunity. Your boy-friend had all three, and so far they haven't turned up anyone else about whom that can be said."

" You make it sound so simple."

But Crook said sharply that murder was never simple, not for the chap who wielded the blunt instrument, the chap at the receiving end or the bighead who thought he knew how to solve crime. He added he thought they'd got as far as they could until he'd seen his new client.

" Don't expect him to be a good witness," Rupert said in warning tones. " He's madder than a March hare having his plans upset as it is."

" That's what I can't bear to think of," said Juliet simply.

" Torquil of all men incarcerated in a little box—he really could go out of his mind."

Crook snorted. " I wouldn't give much for a mind that couldn't shelter me for a few days or weeks, when things went wrong. Who does he think he is ? The Lord God ? And look at it this way. I've known times when innocent men were safer in prison than anywhere else. Y'see, once it gets around that the firm of Crook and Parsons are on the warpath X is goin' to start gettin' restive. The advantage of knowing such a lot of chaps who don't respect the law the way they should is you can generally find someone to give you a hand at a pinch. And even puttin' out my light wouldn't frank X, because that still leaves Bill, and I'm a sucking-dove compared with Bill when his blood's up. But say Torquil was found in the river or on a railway embankment and it seemed like suicide, well, X is going to take such a deep breath of relief there ain't going to be much air left in the neighbourhood for anyone else. No, no, he'll be getting waited on better than he's done for years from all I can hear, and he's got me to do his worrying for him, so if he's dissatisfied he's a difficult customer indeed."

The three took that for a curtain line and stood up. Rupert produced an envelope and pushed it across the table. " Retaining fee," he muttered.

" Very handsome," acknowledged Crook. " Been robbing a bank or do the refugees stump up for their champion ? "

" You won't split on us to Tork, will you ? " said Rupert, anxiously. " He's such a madman he'd be quite capable of calling it misappropriation of funds." And not the only one, Crook reflected, watching them go, pouring themselves into something that looked like a green tin cart. But it moved off as smoothly as the Superb herself and we all know beauty is only skin deep.

When Bill heard of their latest assignment he said, " I don't know whether there are more nut cases now than there used to be or if it's just that the nuts latch on to you, but thank heaven for a few real wrong 'uns like Harry Morgan. They do revive your faith in human nature."

" When you try bein' cynical, Bill, it's like an elephant

trying to do embroidery," Crook informed him. "Me, I never did care about loose ends and this is my chance to sew up the Aslett case. Now I'm off to see my new clients, so say your prayers, Bill, because I have an idea we're going to need 'em."

CHAPTER VIII

"RAINCOAT ?" SAID TORQUIL vaguely. "Oh well, if Ruth saw me wearing it when I went into the Casbah obviously I couldn't have left it in a telephone booth. Most likely I left it on the floor of the coffee bar, though possibly I laid it on the parapet of the bridge on my way home."

"Do you normally stand about on bridges in the heart of a fog ?" inquired Crook, not caustically but because he really wanted to know.

"I didn't expect to be seeing it again for some time, at all events," Torquil explained, and Crook realised for the first time that this expedition he had so much at heart could spell danger to the ultimate degree. And he thought Torquil had a quality of liveness (he couldn't think of a substitute word) that marked him out from all the rest of his gang. Him and me 'ud make a good pair, he thought.

"If you really left it there you can probably say good-bye to it," was all he answered. The sort of chap who'd be hanging about on Westminster Bridge in that weather probably never read a paper, and wouldn't appreciate the gravity of the situation if he did. He might be a refugee himself.

He took his man through his tale of the evening's events ; it didn't differ in detail from what he had already told the police.

"You didn't happen to mention that Paul had a brief-case with him ?"

"I didn't think about it. Is it important ? He did have one, as a matter of fact. I remember his grabbing it up. Poor little sod ! He was like a woman, the way he wanted to make the right impression, the right clothes, the right manner. I would never be surprised to know he practised every gesture in front of a glass."

"What was the brief-case like ?"

"Oh, he might have pinched it from a Foreign Office official. I have a plastic job myself I picked up for ten bob at the local Free-for-all, but he took a fancy to have a solid affair. Ruth's fault really, she had one of that kind, it had been her father's or something, and he said why couldn't he have one like it ? It seemed such a silly little thing for a man to want, who'd been through a Revolution —none of us, of course, suspected him then, but Colin Grant, who's a very good-natured chap, offered to get him one—it was second-hand but I suppose it gave him a sense of security." Torquil suddenly passed his hand over his forehead. "When we start talking about Paul I find I still think of him as the man he represented himself to be, and yet he was never a striking sort of chap, the kind you'd recognise if you met him again, I suppose he felt he had to bolster himself up."

"I wouldn't have called him exactly defenceless myself," murmured Crook dryly.

"Certainly not in the last event. I didn't know then about this fellow, Heinz. Paul must have realised the cat was out of the bag with a vengeance and rampaging over the garden wall. So, just to keep the ball rolling, he tried a spot of blackmail. Either I financed him . . ."

"On what scale ?"

"We didn't get that far."

"Or he went to the Press. Did you really think he would ?"

"I was quite sure he would. In fact, I thought he was arranging to burn the candle at both ends, that's why I went after him so fast."

"You're going to be asked what steps you were proposing to take to prevent him selling you out to the Press. Well, come on, how far were you prepared to go ?"

"Not to the pitch of murder. I've never seen any good come out of violence yet, and I did my National Service in a part of the world where chaps of my age (though admittedly not my nationality) were under orders to bury prisoners alive. I don't say I'd have risked my life on thin ice to save Paul from drowning, but I certainly wouldn't have hit him over the head with a brick. For one thing," he added in less heated tones, " it would have the worst possible effect on our work. It may seem a pretty minor affair to you, Mr. Crook, but I've given the job five years of my life, and I'm prepared to give it another twenty-five, if I can hope to accomplish anything. And now that little rat . . ."

" You're not at Speakers' Corner now," Crook reminded him. " And you haven't answered my question. Say you had found Paul that night what were you going to do ? "

" Stop him selling his yarn to the Press."

" I thought you'd already tried that."

" Isn't it a penal offence to pass yourself off as someone else and milk the public while you're doing it."

" So you were going to yank him along to the police station ? "

" In the final event."

" Only you didn't find him and you didn't go to the police. You came home and started packing."

" When I couldn't locate him in any of the local call-boxes, I thought this was another bluff, and I'd wait and call it. He'd given me till noon the following day."

" To get in touch. But you didn't try, did you ? "

" I felt pretty certain the mountain would come to Mahomet. There's a law of libel and even the Press don't like sticking their necks out too far."

" Don't you believe it," Crook told him grimly. " The Press is like a giraffe." And then he said, " Who were the chaps who were expected to make bricks without straw ? " And Torquil told him courteously, " The Israelites."

" At least they had Moses to frank them," recalled Crook. " But you—you believe in doing things the hard way, don't you ? " And he added, " If you didn't organise your association a bit more skilfully than you manage your own private affairs, it's surprising to me you haven't been in

Queer Street before this. Did you mention your meeting with Paul to a single soul?"

"I didn't see anyone after I left the Casbah."

"The next morning—Saturday—before Oakapple came visiting—had you done anything?"

"I told you—I was waiting for Paul to telephone."

"You really believed he would?"

"At all events he hadn't made the morning papers, and since none of the Press lads had come bumbling round my address I decided he was playing a waiting game, too. I don't want to sound big-headed," he added in a very serious voice, "and I'm nothing special myself, but some of my relations would vomit up their souls to see their pictures in the Press. A very blue-nosed lot, haven't spoken to me since I started on this job."

Crook, who did few things by halves, had already checked up his newest client in Debrett, and realised that the late Aslett might have netted quite a nice little sum if he'd turned his blackmailing attention towards that field. He supposed they consoled themselves as best they could with the thought that every flock has its black sheep, and at the rate he was going he'd be lucky to last beyond his thirtieth birthday.

"There's more ways of killing a baby than smothering it," he observed, causing his companion to start violently. "Likewise there's more ways of committing suicide than putting a bullet through your brain."

On the way out he asked the warder, to whom his name was as familiar as that of the Royal Family, if any of Torquil's bang-up relations had surfaced, but he got the answer he anticipated.

"For all Thy mercies, O My God," he chanted, getting into the Superb and driving away like Jehu. At least there wouldn't be a family to start pricking him from behind, like a devil with a three-pronged fork. He rather expected the two girls in the case to do all that was necessary in that direction.

"Break, break, break," he sighed, bouncing into his Bloomsbury Street office. "That brook didn't know its luck, Bill. The only thing that's likely to break in this case is my heart."

But in point of fact, a break of a very different kind was on the way.

: : : :

Sam Barnard was a small-part actor who, on the night of the murder, was booked to travel by charter night flight to Rome, where a film company was making a picture called *Steps of Desire*, the background clearly being the famous Spanish Steps of that city. Barnard had been S O S'd when the original actor had slipped on the aforesaid steps and broken his leg, and it was of pre-eminent importance that he shouldn't miss the plane. He had been spending the evening with his sister and her husband in Chatterley Road, about ten minutes' walk from Brandon Street Station. He was explaining how lucky he was to have got a vacant booking on a charter plane—B.E.A. could offer him nothing for two days—the drink went round and so did the hands of the clock, and suddenly it was time to go. Only then, believe it or not, did any of the three realise the density of the night beyond the window.

" You're going to be lucky if you get a taxi in this," the brother-in-law opined.

" Oh nonsense ! Nobody else will be out." That was Hilda, already spinning the dial. But none of the local taxi ranks so much as answered, and when she tried two or three car hire firms in the neighbourhood the reply was always the same. Thank you very much but they had no cars for hire that evening, they were all out.

" Better make for the subway station," said the brother-in-law. " Too bad about my car. Some moron lurched into it and tore off a bumper and left one of the wheels looking the same shape as a coolie's hat."

Hilda rang the airways office in Hilary Street. Passengers were conveyed from there to one of the minor airports by the company's own buses ; she was told they couldn't hold up the bus, they were likely to be delayed in any case by the weather.

" One of these nasty little men who's got power for the

first time in his life," commented Hilda, briefly. "You'd better hurry, Sam. One thing, the trains will still be running."

Sam's trouble was he wasn't sure how to find Hilary Street when he got off the train; but he hastened down the road and as he approached the station he saw what for an instant he thought must be a mirage, a taxi standing by the kerb. He shouted incredulously, and saw the FOR HIRE sign suddenly flash up, as the cab moved forward.

"I told the chap I had to catch this plane come hell or high water," he explained to Crook. "He said he wouldn't make the trip for a basket full of monkeys, he was going home, and home meant the Portobello Road. I had to offer him a fiver before he'd agree, and even then he wasn't keen. But he hadn't had much of an evening, people staying at home stuck round the telly, and he said if he didn't get back in good time his wife would give him hell, but if she found out he'd turned down five pounds, she'd still give him the full treatment—whatever Sid does is wrong, he said—anyway, he pocketed the fiver and off we went. I must say he knew his onions, I wouldn't have cared to be driving in that weather myself. But he made it with ten minutes to spare. And, of course," he added humorously, "when we got to the airport we had to hang around for nearly three hours before they'd let us go up."

"Would you know this character again?" asked Crook.

"Here, you're asking something, aren't you?"

"You must have had quite a chat with him," Crook insisted.

"In the heart of a fog at eleven p.m.? All I saw was a great red face under a squashed flat cap, and moustaches like a walrus."

"And the inevitable fag?" completed Crook.

"Well, no, he didn't smoke. I offered him my case, but he said he'd given it up. Just as well, he'd have set fire to that thatch before he was half-way through."

"Been to the police with your story?" Crook inquired.

And Barnard said no. "Bit tricky really. I mean, I didn't see any English papers when we were in Rome.

Didn't suppose I'd be missing much. Then when I got back Hilda—my sister—said, 'Men! What they miss! You must almost have seen the murderer.' Meaning the chap in the stained coat."

"We don't know he was the murderer," objected Crook.

"You may not, but my sister does. Well, I got to thinking. I didn't even see this chap, Fenner, though I dare say he was there, I didn't really see anything but the taxi, and I wasn't sure I saw that. Only—if he'd been parked there for more than a minute or so you'd expect him to have seen this character when he came bouncing out of the alley."

"Could be he did."

"He hasn't come forward."

"Could be he had his reasons."

"I read up the report on the case, Hilda had kept all the cuttings, she's always on at me and Herbert, that's my brother, to write a crime play for television, and one of these days he'll probably do it, and I put on my thinking cap. Then I heard you were taking a hand, so I thought I'd come along and have a word."

"And a very good idea," said Crook heartily. "The police are under-staffed and overworked, you can't open a newspaper or turn a radio knob without hearing that, and seeing you don't know who the driver was or why he ain't surfaced, why go bothering them when I'm around to bear the burden in the heat of the day?"

"Meaning you can pull a string or two?" suggested Barnard.

Crook cocked his big red head. "Never been able to be of service to you?" he hazarded. "Don't often forget a face."

"Remember a chap called Henry Bryce? Yes, I can see you do. If they let him give evidence on your behalf at Judgment Day you'll be wafted through the Golden Gates no holds barred."

Crook reflected that kind words are better than nothing, and nothing was just what he'd been able to collect from the unfortunate Bryce. In reply to Barnard's earlier suggestion he said blandly, "Bill has a lot of useful connections, even if they don't have handles to their names. If he'd opted for the police we might hear less about their troubles. Now, I've got your address just for emergencies, and I may say that if all my witnesses told their stories as well as you my job 'ud be a lot easier. Still, any time I can help . . ." He beamed. "Tell you what I'll do. When that film of yours comes round to the local I'll go and see it in person."

"That's big of you, Mr. Crook." Barnard's voice was full of enthusiasm and Crook saw it was the real McCoy. This chap knew, if lots of others didn't, that, in his profession, if silence is golden, time is the same gold encrusted with diamonds.

When Bill looked in to say, "Any soap?" Crook replied promptly: "The best-scented. Bill, put out some inquiries for a driver called Sid, living Portobello way, big moustache, probably owns his own cab, and when he's found ask him why he's kept his mouth shut all this time—that is, since the night Aslett got his quietus."

Because Barnard was right. If the cab had been stationary for even two or three minutes, the driver could have seen someone going up the passage, and even in a fog he could tell if it was male or female, and possibly a bit more than that.

Bill put a man called Wetherby on to the inquiring end, and pretty soon this man came up with a story of a cab-driver who'd been involved in a bit of trouble on the night of the fog, ran into a stationary vehicle without lights, and broken his wrist, to say nothing of a cut or two on the face. He was now attending hospital as an out-patient and presumably drawing sick benefit. His address was Anselm Street, a pebble's throw from the famous market.

"Good enough," said Crook and, believing that when you want a thing done it's usually good sense to do it yourself, he tooled himself round the same evening. A woman who was presumably Sid's wife opened the door and regarded her visitor with instant suspicion.

"What is it?" she demanded. "He's in no state to be bothered. He's got enough on his mind as it is."

"Give him my card," coaxed Crook, and she took it reluctantly.

"You're not the police?"

"Do I look like the police? Anyway, is he expecting them?"

"I don't know what he's expecting and that's a fact." She left him in the little hall. An instant later she came out and beckoned him into a room at the end of the passage.

"Hi, Sid," said Crook. "I gather you were expecting the rozzers...."

"Don't know who told you that," said Sid.

"Feel up to answering a few questions? Mind you, you know your rights as a citizen of the freest country on earth. Only, if it ain't me, it might be them."

"Look, Mr. Crook," Sid begged, "I dunno what you're getting at."

"In another minute you'll be telling me you never heard of me."

"Seeing the number of chaps I've brought to your place after dark," Sid began.

"Didn't happen to bring one the night of the call-box murder, I suppose?"

"No, Mr. Crook. Not that night."

"Not that you were far off. Stalled in front of Brandon Street Station. That's where Mr. Barnard picked you up, isn't it?"

"I don't know about the name...."

"But a chap did hail you and get you to drive him to the airline office in Hilary Street. Don't say you've forgotten. Shock and a broken wrist ain't the same as concussion, and Mr. B. 'ud know you again."

"He's got nothing against me, Mr. Crook."

"Sure he hasn't. Full of your praises, getting him there in time. Worth every penny of the five quid he gave you."

"If a chap offers me a fiver I've got a right to accept, I suppose? I'm my own boss...."

"Don't let the local council hear you. Nobody's allowed to be his own boss any more. Now, question one coming up. What were you doing standing outside the Underground station at eleven o'clock of a black foggy night ? And don't tell me you were getting a cuppa from an invisible coffee stall because the minute Sam Barnard yelled you put on your light and rolled up like the incomin' tide."

" I was on my way home. I told him."

" You don't live in the station, I suppose ? "

" Well, of course not." Sid was beginning to feel like a poor little bird trying to keep its perch on the bough while a great rogue elephant thrashes about below, intent on rooting up the whole tree.

" But you stopped there. Come on, Sid, let's have the gen. Who were you waiting for ? "

" 'Oo says I was waiting for anyone ? I'd just stopped to light a fag. . . ."

" Don't give me that. You don't smoke. You told Sam Barnard so and anyway, seeing you in your own home surroundings, I could tell that for myself. Now, it's against the law to park flat outside the station, and don't ask me to believe you'd gone along to the gents; because I know that part of the world better than I know my own face, and you'd have gone to the one in the street behind the post office. I suppose you hadn't stopped to put a call through from the box in Brandon Passage ? "

" I get enough gab on that radio in the cab not to want to have any more. Anyway, we don't have the phone."

" So maybe you were waiting for a fare who did want to phone ? Come on, Sid, let's have it. If it ain't me it'll be the bluebottles, I've warned you already, and they might think it odd you hadn't gone to them of your own free will."

" I couldn't tell them anything," cried Sid. " I never saw 'im before. And anyway 'e was on'y going to ring up this club place."

" Who was he ? " asked Crook.

" 'Ow the 'ell do I know ? Just one of those blokes with more money than sense—well, you wouldn't catch anyone that had their head screwed on right going there in the first place."

" What's there ? "

Sid looked at him morosely, but Crook saw he wasn't going to try and hold anything back. His own reputation of always wanting to go one better than the police had won him innumerable confidences from men who are stupid enough not to believe a policeman is the working man's best friend.

" Come to think of it, I dare say you might know the place yourself," he allowed. " It's called Fiddlers' Rest, in what they call Chelsea. . . ."

" And you and me, being old-fashioned, call Fulham. Yeah, I know the place though probably not nearly so well as the rozzers. Calls itself a club, new members welcome on presentation of note-case, cheques not accepted, no other references required."

" Drunk as a lord 'e was," Sid continued. " I don't mind telling you I didn't fancy 'im as a fare, but like a fool I hadn't covered my flag and I was cruising, see, and it's not like the war when you could say you hadn't got the petrol. 'E said 'e'd make it worth my while and 'e wanted to go to Perivale Chambers, which ain't too far from here, so I said O.K., but I couldn't take him no farther than Notting Hill Gate Station and 'e could do the rest on Shanks's mare or all-fours, whichever 'e preferred."

" Very neatly put," approved Crook. " And so ? "

" Well, in 'e got and off we went, but we weren't no farther than the station when he started tapping on the glass. Tap, tap, sent me bonkers, as if the fog wasn't enough. I slid back the window and said, ' Sit still, can't you, you bloody great bee ? '—like I told you, he was half as high as Everest—' If you've changed your mind and don't think I know my job, that's O.K. by me,' I said. ' Get out and walk and be damned.' "

" I do like to see an independent spirit in a man," said Crook enthusiastically. " What did he say ? "

" He said, ' I've been robbed. My wallet's gone.' I said, ' Can't you think up something a bit more original than that ? ' He began to howl, ' You gotter take me back, there was twenty pounds in that wallet.' And then something about his wife giving it him."

" The wallet ? Or hell ? " asked Crook, absorbed.

" To tell you the truth, Mr. Crook, I don't know and I don't care, but this I will say. There may have been twenty quid in his blooming wallet when he got to the Fiddlers' Rest, but if he had twenty bob left when he came out, Joe's losing his touch."

" Joe ? " Mr. Crook wouldn't have missed this conversation for a basketful of monkeys.

" Joe Francis, him that runs the place. Not that I've ever been there myself. Well, stands to reason, they have to be a bit careful and an honest man 'ud ruin their reputation. ' Now, look,' I told him—he was creating like nobody's business—' you could have dropped it in the street or something, you don't want to go the whole way back, why don't you hop out and phone ? There's a box in the passage.' Mind you, I don't think 'e believed me, but anyway 'e went, I could 'ear him reeling around."

" And then this chap, Barnard, came down Penton Street and hailed you and you kissed your fare sweet Fanny Adams and were on your way ? There's a saying about being off with the old love before you're on with the new, or had you forgotten ? "

Sid was looking pretty down in the mouth. " Strewth, Mr. Crook, they could have my licence for this."

" And you'd be getting off easy at that," said Mr. Crook heartlessly. " So that's the last you saw of him ? "

" Yes," said Sid. He thought an instant and said, " Yes," again.

" Maybe you heard something," suggested crafty Mr. Crook.

" I couldn't say if it was 'im, sounded more like a cat. There's times when I think cats get the best of it," brooded Sid darkly.

" What did you hear ? "

" Kind of a screech, I dunno, you know how cats are. I said as much to the American gent. Some cat's having a good time, I said."

" Now, think hard, Sid. You didn't hear any words ? "

" What, all that way off ? "

" The sound couldn't have been a yell, something that suggested a man was in danger ? "

" I told you, Mr. Crook, I thought it was a cat. Why shouldn't it have been ? "

" If someone came up behind you and hit you on the head with a lump of brick, what kind of a noise do you think you'd make ? "

" But why, Mr. Crook ? That's what I keep asking myself. I mean, it's a long way from having a few over the eight to smashing in a chap's skull."

" Maybe if you'd waited for him he'd have told you."

" I'd 'ad enough, Mr. Crook, and that's the truth. It was a mistake takin' 'im to start with—'e couldn't 'ave got me into trouble, 'e couldn't 'ave seen well enough to read my number if 'e 'adn't been loused up—and I waited a minute or so, two or three, I dare say. 'E might 'ave been 'aving me on right through, mightn't e' ? I mean, he could have known about the kiosk and pretended to be phoning, and all the time that was as far as he wanted to go."

" I know this is the Welfare State and we never had it so good," Crook agreed. " But it sounds to me a lot of work to do for a matter of five bob. You'll have to think up something better than that, Sid. You don't remember, of course, what time it was when you shed him ? "

" It was nigh eleven when I picked him up. I said, ' My day ends at eleven,' and he said something about it wasn't eleven yet."

" Sober enough to look at his watch ? "

" The Bluejacket on the corner stops open till eleven now they've got the extra half-hour, and the lights were on there, even through the fog you could see 'em. . . ."

" A very good point," said Crook judiciously. " Could you have reached Brandon Street Station by eleven o'clock ?"

" 'Ave a 'eart, Mr. Crook. You know what the fog was like that evening. . . ."

" So you'd put it at—what ? Five past ? Ten ? "

" Well, it was about the quarter when the American gentleman hailed me, and I'd been waiting about five minutes like I said. . . ."

" And Mr. Fenner bears out your story. Don't worry, Sid, so far as I'm concerned you're in the clear. Your fare—don't know his name, of course? No. And I dare say if he gave one at the Fiddlers' Rest it wouldn't be one his wife would recognise—may have been a nasty bit of work, but I don't think it was him gave the man of mystery his quietus."

" You going to the police, Mr. Crook ? "

" I've been called a lot of things, but never a blackleg. They wouldn't thank me for interfering. The chap who could make trouble for you is your deserted fare and he don't seem to have surfaced. Oh well, has his own reasons, I dare say. I wouldn't want to be the one to explain away the bloodstains on an abandoned raincoat. That's a last point, I suppose you don't remember what he was wearing? "

" I'll tell you no lie, Mr. Crook. I don't. Some kind of coat, light-coloured, but no hat, hung on to the cab with both hands. And 'is breath ! "

" And you wouldn't know him again ? "

Sid shook his head. " I'm sorry, Mr. Crook."

" You getting enough to eat ? " asked Crook. " I mean, sick benefit and all that. I should think you could do with a bit of feeding up."

He slipped a folded note under a plaster Alsatian dog, reflecting that it was no improvement on the ribbon fern in its china pot of his young days.

" Well, thanks, Mr. Crook," said Sid, and Crook knew the thanks weren't chiefly for the folded note.

" Thanks to you," Crook corrected. " Anything I can ever do for you . . ."

" I'll remember that, Mr. Crook."

Crook grinned. " You married chaps are all the same." He turned at the door. " By the way, I take it you didn't see anyone else while you were hanging about ? Nobody came out of the passage ? "

" I didn't see anyone, Mr. Crook, and that's the truth."

" I believe you," said Crook. He was remembering the steps he had heard moving away from the phone booth. Most likely went straight on past the booth and came out in Manders Street. Not likely to run into anyone there, there's no show on at the Palace at the moment, and there's a second entrance to the Underground nearby, he could have nipped down. . . . That left Fenner. But Barnard had surfaced at practically the same time, so it was quite probable that Sid hadn't seen the little chap.

He was as pleased with this development as a child who, having planted a packet of seeds, goes down one fine morning to find the first green shoots pricking through the earth.

" Be seeing you, Sid," he promised. " And meanwhile, be good to yourself."

He told Mrs. Sid that her husband was doing champion.

Mrs. Sid sniffed. " It's not your wrist. Cracked his ribs, too," she added, for good measure, " whatever that doctor may think, Sid asked if he could have them bound just to ease him like, and the young chap at the hospital said, ' Oh, we don't bind them any more, you just go home and bear it.' "

" Nice to see a sensible chap taking the doctor's advice," Crook offered.

CHAPTER IX

He bowed himself out, merry as a May morning.

Bill was hard at it in Bloomsbury Street when he came bouncing in to report progress. A bit later he went out again.

" If I don't get back around my usual time, send the rozzers to investigate any ditches, cellars or attics at the Fiddlers' Rest."

" You ought to wear wellingtons if you're going to wade through that muck," said Bill nonchalantly.

Crook said he must see about getting himself a pair, though not to-day, and went off again.

He found the night-club without any difficulty ; like so many establishments of its kind it seemed to operate mainly from the underground. Getting inside was quite another matter. A short slight man with a yellowish complexion and about as much intelligence as a bull (non-pedigree) came to the door in reply to his imperious thudding.

"We are not open," he said. It amused Crook to note how his voice changed in midstream as it were; it started by being almost conciliatory but even he couldn't see a possible client in Arthur Crook, and it ended on a note approaching insolence.

"I can see that for myself," the lawyer replied. "You should call it the After Dark Club. I want to speak to your boss."

"He is not here."

"I'll come in and wait."

"No." The door began to close.

"It's me or the police," said Crook amiably. "You can take your choice."

"The police have nothing on Mr. Francis."

"That's what you think, buddy."

He'd made a few inquiries, with Bill's invaluable help, and he knew that Mr. Francis hadn't been born that way. More like Mr. Frankelfurter, he reflected.

"I don't know who you are," the man complained, but the door didn't close any farther.

"That's your loss," said Crook. He fished out one of his enormous unconventional cards and passed it over.

"You wish for membership?" inquired the little yellow man doubtfully.

"You want a punch on the boko?" asked Crook, inelegantly. "I do my drinking decent. Go on, find the boss."

A voice from the darkness in the passage beyond asked a question. The door closed promptly, and Crook leaned placidly against the wall. He couldn't hear what was going on within but he could imagine it all right. Little Chinkee might be ignorant of the caller's identity but Crook hadn't a doubt that Francis would recognise the name. And he was right. The door opened, a surly voice invited him to enter, and he stepped into a brightly-painted, cheerful passage with a sort of counter, presumably for checking up members and their friends. Mr. Francis was tall and eagly, if you can imagine a corrupt and partially desiccated eagle. Actually he reminded Mr. Crook of a man who'd been a great theatrical star in his (Crook's) youth and had been gathered to his fathers some years since. But this was the kind of part he'd been wont to play.

" Mr. Crook ? " said this apparition, not offering his hand. " I don't know you, I believe."

" You will." He looked into the big basement club room. Everything clean and gay here, too, just a place where the nice boys could bring their nice girls, that's what it looked like on the surface. Crook smiled angelically. " Where's the rest of it ? "

" The rest ? "

" Where the lonely gentlemen can meet the little girls ? or the little boys, come to that ? Never mind, don't tell me. I ain't the police. All I'm here for is to get back a wallet belonging to a client."

" A wallet ? I know nothing. . . ."

" Then perhaps you can suggest who does. This client of mine—no names, no pack drill, or would you prefer . . . ? "

" We don't inquire into our members' private affairs," said Mr. Francis.

" And I dare say the names they write in your book wouldn't tally with the ones on their passports. I get you. Now, listen. This client of mine was here on the night of the 14th. He left shortly before eleven, either he'd drunk his way through a lake, or you serve a special inflammatory brand. Again, I'm not interested. I stick to beer myself." He saw the pained look on Mr. Francis's face. " He left his wallet behind him, and I want it back."

" Really, Mr. Crook . . ."

" Really, Mr. Francis. I'm not interested in the contents of the wallet, but I want the thing itself. I dare say if you were to ask among your lady hostesses one of them might recall a careless client. . . ."

" If the wallet had been found on the premises it would have been handed over," the corrupt eagle insisted.

"Then maybe it wasn't found. Maybe it was just removed. No dice? O.K., let me shake another ace out of my sleeve. You've read about the Phone Box Murder?"

"I think so."

"So you know that a man wearing a bloodstained coat was seen by a witness about the time Luzky (so-called) got his chips?"

"I do not follow the details of every sordid crime——"

"Don't blame you," said Crook. "You must be up to your ears here—still, maybe it was an error to bypass this one. Y'see, the chap that found the corpse had just left your premises."

"And—if one may ask—what is your interest in the affair, Mr. Crook? You represent the alleged owner of the wallet?"

"I represent the chap they've taken for the murder. And I've contacted the driver who picked up the owner outside."

"I should have guessed. This taxi-driver—most convenient. How much does his evidence set you back—or should I say, set your client back?"

"Nothing to what that last remark's going to cost you. Might even shut your club down. Of course, if you can't help me, my witness will go to the police and they'll come along. . . ."

"I can tell them no more than I have told you."

"They won't start with questions," Crook assured him. "They'll just go right through your membership books and *then* they'll start asking the questions, and the answers better be good."

"Was the wallet made of solid gold?" demanded Mr. Francis. "Or perhaps it contained a thousand pounds?"

"I told you, I'm not interested in the contents. If idiots like to sling their money about in hash-houses like this, that's their funeral and I dare say quite often it's just that, but the wallet's another matter. A wallet's a personal possession that can be identified."

"If one were found it would most likely not be kept."

"No? Suppose your member had come in the next

night and asked for it and suppose he was the sort that was likely to make a stink when it wasn't forthcoming?"

Mr. Francis gave him a smile of infinite corruption. "I do not think that is probable, Mr. Crook."

"You mean, he wouldn't want to advertise the fact that he'd ever set foot in here? I don't blame him. But so long as that wallet isn't in his possession, you see his situation. Well, of course you do. Why, it could be dynamite. And don't tell me again," he said quickly, "that it's been chucked away. These things sometimes have a value that 'ud startle the chap who sold them in the first place."

"And if I tell you I know nothing of any trumpery wallet . . ."

"I shall advise my client to go to the police."

The corrupt eagle hesitated; he thought it highly improbable Crook would do anything of the sort. Only fools try to implicate the police in their affairs, if it means wading through an Augean stable like the Fiddlers' Rest, and whatever Crook was it wasn't a fool. All the same, there are chances no man outside an asylum cares to take. He debated.

Crook watched him, seeing these thoughts pass through his mind like goldfish in a bowl. "You know what they say," he observed to Bill later, "what you don't know don't hurt you. What you don't know don't help you either. Eagle-Face only had to say, 'Yes, I remember the wallet, it was sent back next day, I have the record in my book,' and I'd have been stymied. Of course, I could still have dragged the police in, but think what that would have done to my reputation. Might as well put up the shutters and queue up at the Home for Distressed Non-Gentlefolk. Talk about the lion lying down with the lamb. This little lamb would have been put in the pot and boiled till he was done the same week-end."

At last Mr. Francis said grudgingly, "I will see if a wallet is among the unclaimed property found on the premises. If you will describe it . . ."

"I'll do better than that," promised Crook, "I'll come

right along with you. If you feel you need a bodyguard, bring Chu Chin Chow along."

Though actually the chap who needed a bodyguard here was himself, so he added, "And if he's got a knife up his sleeve and he happens to stumble against me in the dark with fatal results, my partner's all set to take over, in which case you'd be well-advised to give your undertaker due notice."

The two men, followed by the little yellow shadow, made their way down a passage into a much darker part of the house. Crook got the fantastic idea that the cupboard, which was tall and narrow, was, in effect, a coffin and choked back a chuckle to think how badly he'd fit it. Mr. Francis put the key in the lock and opened the door about a foot, interposing his body between the contents and his maddening visitor whom he likened in his mind to a germ of some malignant disease. Crook, however, simply pulled a pencil torch out of his pocket and shone it under the tall man's arm.

The torch-beam lighted up the wallet immediately. It was a beauty all right, green morocco leather soft enough for a princess to sleep on, with a gilt initial in one corner.

"That's it," he declared, indicating it.

"And your client's name, Mr. Crook?"

"We-ell," said Crook, "if he didn't give it to you of his own free-will, he wouldn't thank me for making you a present of it."

"Really, Mr. Crook, you cannot imagine I am going to hand this over to you with no proof that you are even acting for the owner?"

"I'll give you a receipt," Crook offered.

"And when the gentleman makes inquiries and hears that I have parted with it—what is my position then?"

"Fair enough," agreed Crook. "O.K., you parcel it up and get Chu Chin Chow to take it down to the post office. Registered post, mark you, and I'll be a witness that it was sent. Don't let your feelings be hurt that I won't take your word that you'll post it back the minute I've gone. In my racket you get so as you wouldn't believe the Angel

Gabriel wasn't a Mephistopheles in disguise, doing a take-over bid. You don't like my suggestion? O.K., here are two alternatives. Ring the police and tell them you've got the thing and have any inquiries been made, or ring your client and ask him if I'm on the level."

"We do not ask our clientele for their telephone numbers, Mr. Crook."

"Might be surprised at what you got if you did. Still, I take it he'd be in the book?"

Mr. Francis said nothing.

"I get you. Not under the name he's using here."

"Our clients are referred to by number," said Mr. Francis.

"How convenient!" Crook applauded. "Too bad H.M. Prison Service thought up the idea before you did. Well, we're luckier, our clients don't mind giving us phone numbers, so if you'll let me have the use of your phone—he stuck his great hand into his pocket and produced four coppers—I'll get on to Bill and tell him to latch on to our client."

"Why do you not ring your client yourself?"

"Because if I did that and let him know where I was speaking from, he wouldn't be my client much longer. Besides, I don't remember his number off-hand. But it'll be on the file and Bill can contact him. . . . Well, if he didn't give you a name he could have his reasons. Chaps like to keep some of their business private. Sometimes it comes expensive being expansive." He roared with laughter at his own deplorable humour. Francis looked as if he'd like to vomit, and plenty of people would have felt just the same. Crook's notions of humour dated from the silent cinema, the days of Mark Lemon and Larry Semon, when custard pies were all the rage, and he couldn't see any reason why he should change his style.

He lifted the telephone receiver and dialled his office number.

"Hi, Bill. Speaking from the Fiddlers' Rest. They've got You-Know-Who's wallet, but they won't part, not without his say-so. Now, can you get in touch—the number's on the file—and ask him either to come down here or ring Mr. Francis and tell him to hand it over ? If you can't get him ring me back and I'll call the rozzers. No, I'll be here as long as the wallet is." He hung up.

" My client will appreciate your thoughtfulness," he told Mr. Francis. " Well, you don't want the police nosing into your affairs and nor does he. And seeing the wallet was a present from a lady . . ." He took it suddenly out of the tall man's hands and flapped it open. Whatever it had once contained it was empty now. Still, no man with a head on his shoulders would carry his identity card in a place like this. Crook, who knew a lot about such establishments, decided it catered to a large extent for the well-lined provincial up for some trade exhibition or annual meeting, minus the wife, finding himself at a loose end and encountering by chance, in a bar most likely, some friendly chap who happened to have heard of the Fiddlers' Rest and why not go along and have a drink or two ? Nice little girls (he still wasn't sure about the little boys, but the place had a sinister reputation) and it wouldn't surprise him to learn that Mr. Francis Frankelburger ran a nice side-line in blackmail.

The telephone rang. Chu Chin Chow answered it.

" For Mr. Crook," he announced sullenly.

Francis took a couple of swift steps and picked up a second receiver hanging against the dark wall.

Crook waited politely for him to get set. Then, " Crook speaking. From the Fiddlers' Rest. They've got the wallet so let's have your instructions and have 'em fast. I don't want to die of the mephitic plague."

A deep voice said in desperate tones, " Mr. Crook, for God's sake get it back. Tell them I won't make any trouble, bring any charge or ask what's happened to the contents. I just want the wallet back."

" Have a word with Mr. Francis," Crook offered.

He waited, inwardly on tenterhooks, in case his bluff should be called. In a reasonable State, he reflected, he'd be allowed to jump on this thug and collect the wallet by force, and if he did Francis probably wouldn't dare call in the police. Or he could himself threaten to go round to the nick, but if he did you could be dead sure that when the authorities called at the Fiddlers' Rest there'd be no sign of a wallet, with Francis and Chu Chin Chow both swearing themselves blue in the face they'd never set eyes on any such thing.

The deep voice was still cajoling, instructing. Crook hoped Bill wouldn't overdo it, then reflected that he hadn't let his boss down in twenty-five years and wasn't likely to start now.

All the same it was a relief when he heard Francis say, " If Mr. Crook will give me a receipt he may take the wallet. But I accept no responsibility once it has left my premises."

Crook signed the receipt like a bird, heaved a gusty sigh and got back into the Old Superb. Bill knew his onions, he thought, he'd almost persuaded Crook that he knew the owner of the wallet—and with Bill on the trail Crook hadn't the least doubt that in a very short time they would.

Then and only then could Crook hope to put the bite on.

CHAPTER X

" A NICE JOB," said Bill appreciatively, turning the wallet over in his sensitive hands. " Did Sid say the wife gave it to him ? Odds are then it's British workmanship. At a guess I'd say there are four manufacturers at most who'd turn out a lush job like that. I'll get a man on to it."

" Keep Wetherby on the job," said Crook. " He can go the rounds. He doesn't have to say he represents the police, but if they happen to get that idea—well, there's no harm done."

" Give him 24 hours," said Bill confidently. " He'll come home with the bacon."

" We only take the best here," Crook reminded him.

It irked him to reflect that any minute now he'd have to take the police into his confidence unless Torquil was to stay in prison indefinitely.

Wetherby brought home the bacon in slightly under the 24 hours allotted to him. The wallet had been made by a firm called Pascoe to order for a Mrs. A. Gordon ; she had explained it was a tenth wedding anniversary gift for her husband. The anniversary had taken place some months earlier.

" I've got Gordon's address," Wetherby went on. " He's quite a big bug in the City, though a lot of that is due to father-in-law's influence. Said father-in-law sits on about forty boards and I'd say bought little Alistair for his Fiona."

Crook examined the wallet. " It seems a tasty sort of present to mark ten years in the doghouse. I suppose she hasn't been doing a little coaxing act on the side ? "

" Her folk should have called her Maud," said Wetherby simply. " You remember, icily regular, splendidly null."

" Kids ? " asked Crook, and Wetherby said, " Well, no, they'd all have been born refrigerators."

Alistair Gordon had an office half the size of a palais de danse and a table a quarter of a mile wide, or so it appeared to Crook. At first a very haughty piece called Miss Cameron tried to slap him down saying he couldn't see Mr. Gordon without an appointment. She gave him a form to fill in. He saw there was a line marked Business, so he wrote, " Would you like to know who has your wallet now ? ", folded the form and asked the Iceberg for an envelope. She looked as if she couldn't believe her ears and would like to box his, but she brought him one, at a second glance, and he sealed it carefully with the form inside.

" Take it into the boss," he begged, " and tell him that if he wants to call his lawyer I can wait."

This message penetrated even that ivory dome and she flounced off. It seemed a long time before she came back, but when presently he saw the size of the room he forgave her.

" Mr. Gordon can spare you five minutes," she told him sulkily.

Gordon was about thirty-five, and must have been a handsome figure of a man before marriage with a rich tycoon's daughter drove him to drink and the Fiddlers' Rest. As soon as Crook reached the desk he exclaimed, " Is this a joke, Mr. Crook ? "

" Putting your head in the lion's mouth is never a joke," Crook assured him. " Even to me that makes a habit of it." He took a photograph from his pocket. " I believe the original of this is your property."

Gordon took the photograph, which represented the missing wallet. " Where did you come across this ? " he demanded aggressively.

" You left it at the Fiddlers' Rest on the night of the 14th and don't give me the run around and say you weren't there because it's been identified by the firm that made it."

" But—I telephoned the Fiddlers' Rest the next morning. They assured me no such wallet had been found."

Then his face changed. " What's the wallet to you ? Has my wife . . . ? "

" I've never met the lady. And you shouldn't be surprised if Mr. Francis couldn't remember it. He'd know you can't afford to raise a stink, and so long as they had it—well, it's like a deposit in the Savings Bank, something for a rainy day, and I doubt if the roof of the Fiddlers' Rest would be much help to its members in a storm."

" Is there any sense asking if there was any money in it ? " questioned Gordon.

" None at all," Crook agreed. " Still, count your blessings. I ain't a married man myself, but what I know about the dames 'ud surprise you. And going about with a tin can round your neck saying Totally Blind . . . because you've lost a couple of eyes in a domestic fracas. . ."

" Let's cut the cackle, Mr. Crook," interrupted Gordon, crisply. " What's your price ? "

" Price for what ? "

" The wallet, naturally."

" You don't know the law," expostulated Crook. " I can't sell what ain't mine. And, bein' a lawyer with a certain reputation, I didn't have to pay Joe Francis either."

" You haven't explained yet how you came to be interested in it."

"Didn't I? Oh well, I'm acting for a man called Torquil Holland."

"Wait a minute, I've heard that name, haven't I?"

"Don't play it too smooth," Crook begged. "Of course you've heard it. He's the chap they took for the phone box murder."

"Of course. I remember."

"I'll say. Any special reason you didn't report your find to the police?"

He was an adept at hitting under the belt, and this time he had his man well on the run.

"I don't know what you're talking about."

"Don't come the old innocent over me. I've got the taxi-driver that dropped you at the mouth of the passage and heard you bawl when you opened the door and found the corpse. And don't tell me he deserves to lose his licence, oiling off and leaving you on your tod, because he's about the one chap who can alibi you—him and Fenner, of course."

Gordon seemed temporarily deprived of speech. "It was the driver told me about the wallet and picking you up from the Fiddlers' Rest. I wouldn't say you exactly shed your wallet there, more it was plucked like a flower by a pair of dainty fingers."

"How did you persuade Francis to hand it over?"

"As a matter of fact, he got the idea I was acting for you, and though I ain't exactly his favourite man he'd sooner deal with me than the police. Now, if you don't like the way I'm playing this hand just give your lawyer a tinkle and get him to come right over. I won't run away."

"There's no need to pull him into this."

Crook shook his head unbelievingly. "You don't know you're born. You're going to need all the help you can get, not so much with the police as with your lady wife. I don't say your man of affairs can tell any more truth than you give him, but when it comes to a showdown he'll do it a lot smoother than you. Just mention my name and the sigh that comes over the line will blow all those papers on your desk into the w.p.b." Which, though he charitably refrained from saying so, was probably the best place for them.

Gordon decided to climb down a couple of rungs. "Mr. Crook, is it necessary to drag me into this? I can't help. . . ."

"That's what you think. And as for dragging, you've planted yourself in the very middle of the picture. You're the chap who owns the bloodstained mac, remember, the one you left under the seat in the train."

"That's nonsense," cried Gordon.

"It's a classy article, and it wouldn't surprise me if your tailor recognised it. It got stained with blood, remember? That's what fixed you in Fenner's mind."

"Fenner?"

"The chap outside the subway station."

"He's going to stand up in court and swear to my identity?"

"Well, of course he ain't. Be your age, chum. But he saw a man of round about your build at the time you were dropped at the passage, and he was wearing a bloodstained mac. And don't tell me it was like that when you got into the cab, because Sid wouldn't have taken you at all. I know about the fog, but you had to give him an address and blood ain't exactly inconspicuous, not in that quantity. No, you got those stains after you left the cab—not a trace on the cushions, see—and you don't have to be a dab at Double Your Money to guess they came out of the phone box."

"Look," said Gordon, and now he was so white he might have been made of candle-wax, a horrid transformation of something that hadn't been very agreeable to start with, "don't suppose you can pin this crime on to me. There was no light in the box and when I struck a match there he was, I was practically on top of him. I admit for one moment I thought I was seeing things—Joe's brand of poison would account for almost anything—then I turned and bolted."

"You may have been as tight as an owl," said Crook

unsympathetically, " but even so you must have realised this was a murder, the poor devil couldn't have done that to himself."

" Try and see it my way," Gordon urged. " I'd no proof I wasn't involved—I'd never seen him before, of course, but the police might have argued I'd had a row because he wouldn't let me into the box and I lost my head and picked up a brick. . . ."

" Got a record ? " asked Crook. " I mean, ever been involved in that kind of a shine ? "

" Certainly not."

" And you didn't know the chap ? "

" No."

" So where was the harm calling the rozzers ? Even if you felt too shaken yourself, there was Fenner, like a gift from on high. You only had to say ' Come and look in the box, there's been a case of murder,' and you'd have been all right. The driver could have franked you—come to that," he added casually, " I could have franked you. It's one of those unusual cases where a number of witnesses can pinpoint the time—the man who got your taxi knows exactly when he picked it up, Fenner knows when he came up to the street, and anyway that can be checked by official records—and I happen to know that that murder was committed before 11 o'clock."

Gordon put his hands over his eyes, a gesture, as Crook realised, of sheer incredulous relief.

" You mean, you're prepared to go into the witness-box and say that ? "

" I'm representing Holland. I don't have to go into any witness-box. And anyway I've already told the police. But don't think you're out of the wood. You knew this bloodstained coat didn't belong to my client—and that's the main ground they arrested him on—but you let them go on thinking it was his."

Gordon looked sullen. " He only had to produce his own."

" Which he couldn't do. Left it in some coffee dive of Communist sympathies. And I dare say whoever took it can't afford to tangle with the police . . . you're going to have a spot of explaining to do when it comes to the coat."

" And how do you think you're going to prove it's mine? "

" No objection to a little perjury ? " Crook wondered. " I mean, you're sure to be asked if you ever saw that coat before. And even if you don't recognise it, your wife might know better."

His eye wandered speculatively about the room. In one corner a cupboard had been made to look like part of the panelling. Crook rose abruptly and pulled the door open. A raincoat, stiff as a guardsman and smart as paint, hung on a hook.

" What the devil . . . ? " Gordon began furiously.

But Crook had taken the coat down and was inspecting the label in the neck.

" Direct from head office," he suggested. " These Burberrys are nice jobs, ain't they ? Dare say it wouldn't be too difficult to find out when you bought that, not likely you paid cash, and my guess 'ud be it was the mornin' after the murder. Feel like coming along to the station with me, and makin' a statement ? "

" So you haven't called in on your way ? "

Crook spread his big hands in a theatrical gesture. " I had to see you first," he urged. " Say you hadn't recognised the wallet."

" I still don't understand why you didn't bring it with you instead of that ridiculous photograph. I don't see why you had to have it photographed at all."

" I have to think of my client's interests," Crook pointed out. " Say I give you the wallet, don't ask me to believe Joe Francis is going to come into court and say I got it from him. Not blooming likely. Never set eyes on it, or you, for that matter. Odd, you know. Like the rain falling on the just and the unjust. Innocent or involved, no one wants to tangle with the police if he can help it. And seeing you never gave a name where'd I be ? I'll tell you. The monkey on the stick when the stick breaks. You say you weren't at the Fiddlers' Rest, you never took the taxi, you never lost a wallet, you never went near the phone box and you never set eyes on the mac before. So long as I've got the wallet, it can be identified by Mrs. G. and the firm who made it."

" This photograph doesn't prove you've got the wallet," asseverated Gordon sullenly.

" Doubting Thomas isn't in it with you. O.K., come round to my place this evening, say six o'clock, and I'll show it to you. Then you and me will go along to the station, and you can make a statement, about being the chap with the stained coat. No, of course it won't be any tea-party, but then it's not a tea-party to lie in prison on a murder charge, and at least you won't have to face anything like that. I'll have my partner there to see fair play," he added, encouragingly, " and if you like to bring a chum along there'll be no objection. Only—no knives, no guns."

" I'm not a hoodlum," objected Gordon sharply. " You think you've got me on toast, don't you ? "

" You've got your alternative," Crook pointed out. " You can ring up the police yourself, and accuse me of retainin' your property."

" It could still be a trick," Gordon broke out. " I still don't know you've got it."

" Maybe I should have gone to see Mrs. Gordon ? "

" There must be some way of hushing this up. Surely it'll be enough for the police to say that someone has come forward to identify the mackintosh, so that it can't have been the missing one everyone's on the rampage for. Whose interest will be served by my name being published ? "

" You'll have to fix that with the police," Crook told him, impatiently. " Though the Press 'ull be another thing again. Still, I ain't interested in that part of it. I dare say you can fix it for your business to send you to Persia or somewhere till the dust settles. Well, be seeing you and, of course, if you don't identify the wallet, that'll be just one more headache for the police."

On his way back to Bloomsbury Street he tried to fit himself into Gordon's shoes. Say he rings Joe Francis and tells him to destroy the receipt I gave him, even that wouldn't let him out. We've still got Sid's evidence that he did pick up a chap outside the Fiddlers' Rest. Say he gets Mrs. G. to go along with him and swear it ain't the same wallet, we've still got the firm that made it, and their records 'ull be worth a lot more in the witness-box than Gordon's word, even backed up by his ever-loving. Say he manages to run Sid down while the old boy's teetering along to the local, there's still me and Sam Barnard. Unless he's going to organise a modern Massacre of Glencoe he's like Sterne's starling, who couldn't get out.

At this stage in his meditations the Superb landed him at his own office door, so he couldn't finish his train of thought or he might have remembered that the starling aforesaid wound up by saying, " I *will* get out " and though Gordon mightn't be the stuff of which heroes are made he was probably the equivalent of a starling.

He came into the office to find it empty as a new-made grave and a note from Bill, that read : The fish has surfaced at Folkestone, going down with my net a reference to a blackmailer Crook wanted to have on toast for breakfast, lunch and tea. And now it looked as though a tasty dish of fried fish was on the way. The telephone rang and a strange voice, speaking with a curious agitation, begged the favour of an early appointment.

" I'm in trouble, Mr. Crook."

" You wouldn't be calling me if you weren't. Police know ? "

" They're hounding me."

" It's what they're paid for," Crook pointed out, reasonably. But he made the appointment, he never refused, the time for refusal would be when he'd heard the story and thought the fire too hot even for his incandescent fingers to rescue the chestnuts. He ripped open envelopes and scribbled notes in his indecipherable longhand on the enclosures, and the phone rang and he answered it, and then he rang a few numbers, and around lunch-time he had a pair of visitors. He heard footsteps hesitating in the outer office, where Bill normally strained the catch, and a whisper of voices, so he sang out, " Come right in " and in they came, what a Victorian nanny would have called a sight for sore eyes. They were Julie Ware, straight and slim in dark blue, that made her hair look pure gold, and young Rupert Bowen, looking oddly unlike himself in a sober suit and a tie he could almost have worn to a funeral.

" My old man," explained Rupert, " sent me out on an errand the office boy could have done just as well. So I decided to take as much time over the job as the boy would have done. We have offices in Carton Street," he added.

Crook nodded. " That Bowen ? You didn't say."

" And I'm rehearsing for a commercial TV serial," contributed Julie. " We met quite by accident—I didn't even know you worked round here, Ru—the company's rented the Eglington Theatre for rehearsals," she added explanatorily, " and we thought . . . we thought . . ."

" You thought you'd like to bring a bit of sunshine into the old man's life. I know."

" You said you'd keep us *au courant* with events," Julie pleaded, " and we haven't heard a word."

" I promised to tell you any new developments," amended Crook.

" But surely something's happened ? I know silence is golden but we'd be grateful for even the smallest silver coin."

" Sweet Chance, that turned my thoughts abroad—you must be—what's the word ?—telepathic. I haven't contacted you hitherto because there's been nothing to say, but now I've got something." He looked like the latest version of Cinderella's Fairy Godmother about to wave her wand. The young couple actually looked round as if they expected to see a pumpkin coach materialise before their eyes.

Crook leaned forward. " Hold on to your chairs," he said. " I've got the actual owner of the bloodstained coat."

Juliet looked round. " Where ? "

" Well, not in my pocket," agreed Crook. " But he'll be along this evening round about six. Mind you, he may keep me waiting a little, probably thinks it's *infra dig* to keep a date with a mere attorney, but he'll be along."

" Why ? " asked Julie.

" Because, girlie, I've got something he wants, and this is the only way he can get it."

" Visit our Bargain Basement," said Rupert in rapid tones. " What's he giving you in exchange ? "

" A statement—for the police."

" Lumme ! What you've got must be pretty valuable."

" Only a married man would appreciate its worth."

Juliet broke in impatiently, " Oh, do stop talking in riddles. If you know who he is, Mr. Crook, why is Torquil still in prison ? "

Crook looked at her kindly. " The law ain't like a bird that takes off from the ground and goes non-stop to its destination, it's more like a stopping train really, has to call everywhere on the way, but it gets there in the end. Anyway," he added, " I only contacted this chap, Gordon, this morning." He elaborated.

While Rupert greeted the news with suitable enthusiasm Juliet displayed the ingratitude that in Crook's experience was characteristic of the sex.

" But suppose he says it *isn't* his wallet ? "

" He knows darn well it is. Anyway, there's always Mrs. G. and I don't think little Alistair's any match for her. And even if she did come over to his side, there's still the wallet's makers. No, this is one of those locked room mysteries where there ain't any secret solution. He's right in the net and he knows it."

" Suppose, once he's got it back, he says he must have left it in a taxi or something, would this Francis person back you up ? "

" You don't miss much, do you ? " Crook's voice was openly admiring. " But there's Sid, who drove the taxi, and his passenger, Sam, and this other chap who met Gordon wearing the coat outside the Underground. I'm playing them all on my string like a quadruple yoyo." He did a spirited little bit of acting.

Julie forged on like one of the righteous staggering ahead, looking neither right nor left, towards the perfect day.

" But can you *prove* he murdered Paul ? " she insisted.

Crook turned to Rupert, man to man, philosophic, unsurprised.

"See what I mean about a bird (or a dame) taking off from A. and landing plumb on B. without stopping anywhere *en route*? Never heard this chap's name ten minutes ago, and now can't wait to get weaving on a noose. Now, sugar, read, mark, learn and inwardly digest. It ain't my job to find out who murdered your precious Paul. That's a job for the police, and whatever else I've been called, I'm not a blackleg. You're hiring me to get your chap out of quod, and I'm doing quite nicely, thanks. One of the main planks in the police's platform is this coat aforesaid, and if we have proof that it couldn't have belonged to Torquil Holland, the next step'll be the authorities will start hunting for the key of his cell."

Juliet nodded. "Don't think I'm complaining," she said earnestly, "but I look at it from Torquil's point of view. If the real murderer isn't discovered, there'll be plenty of people who will think for the rest of their lives that he was one of the lucky ones who got off for lack of evidence. And that's not good enough, not for him."

"I only met the boy-friend once," Crook conceded, "unless you count my lightning glimpse at the Duck and Daisy, when he didn't even notice my existence, less than the dust beneath his chariot wheel, that kind of thing—but I can't believe he's ever going to give a button what other people think about him. All he's waiting for is the cage door to fly open and he'll be off to the Back of Beyond like a demented lark."

"Suppose he doesn't come?" suggested Rupert, bluntly.

"He'll come all right. He don't want this story of the wallet noised abroad, and he knows if he don't surface I'll go along to the nick and take not only my story, which can be authenticated, but also the wallet, and then the fat will be in the fire. There's more than one kind of prison," he added, "and if Mrs. G. gets hold of the yarn she'll make Nash Place one of those prisons where you never get any remission for good behaviour. This way there'll be no need to mention the wallet. I don't say it'll be a piece of cake for him, but at least he won't be swallowing a death potion."

"Could it be him?" asked Julie, with a lack of grammar that charmed her listener.

"Never taught you arithmetic at your school?" Crook looked faintly shocked. "How could it be him when the chap was dead by 11 p.m. and the taxi containing Gordon didn't turn up at the station till several minutes after the hour? No, I can give him an alibi for murder. He's in deep enough without that. Withholding essential evidence —they might even try for accessory after the fact. Now, your dad will be wondering what's happened to his office boy, and I've got a chap coming who's going to want me to prove he was in North Shields when the police and three incorruptible witnesses know he was in Covent Garden, so my plate's like the Psalmist's cup, it floweth over. Any of you care to be at the Duck and Daisy at, say, 8.30 to-night, I'll give you my report. And cheer up. There's only one way Gordon can duck what's coming to him, and that's by walking under a bus and I don't think even he's quite desperate enough for that."

"I take it you wouldn't like a witness behind the curtain?" Rupert ventured. "O.K., forget it, Mr. Crook."

"But be careful," insisted Julie. "You're terribly important to us. Torquil depends on you."

"Come on, girl," said Rupert in hurried tones. "Eight-thirty, Mr. Crook, and we'll assemble as many as we can, and we'll buy you a barrel."

They went out, so handsome, trim, and debonair, like the halves of the choicest kind of apple; Crook felt cross. Dames all over, he reflected. Here's Young Lochinvar in all his warpaint, but she has to set her silly heart on that human hedgehog, who'll probably expect her to grow fur, if she ever does get him as far as the altar.

The afternoon went by like wind over a field of wheat, nothing much to show, but perpetual movement. He saw the chap who wanted him to juggle the facts and told him he'd better try the Conjurers' Club; someone else came in to settle an account from a wallet stuffed with pound notes, and how much the Inland Revenue was going to get out of that was anyone's guess, at 4.30 Bill rang through with the news that he should be back first thing next morning, and at 5 p.m. the new contact arrived, in a state of such jitters he nearly fell off his chair.

He was a man called Stoneham, convinced that his wife was trying to poison him.

" With rat poison, Mr. Crook," said the poor little creature, who did indeed resemble some sort of rodent, but a very harmless and helpless one, his nose quivered and his black eyes blinked.

" Tackled her ? " asked Mr. Crook, heartlessly.

" She says that even if it was true I shouldn't have anything to worry about, since it's only fatal to rats."

" Been to the police ? "

Stoneham wrung his little paws. " It's no good. Believe it or not, she's sicked them on to me."

Crook thought in his unregenerate fashion how much more satisfactory it would be to have the lady for his client, he liked a dash of ginger, and though he had nothing against mice, as such, they were apt to be a nuisance, you could put your solid No. 10 hoof on them and crush them without even realising what you were doing. The little chap stayed till 5.45. Crook thought a chap with any *nous* would have waited his opportunity and when he believed he was being given a cup of cold pizen, start yelling the place down, and while she rushed to find him an aspirin he'd switch the cups. But he knew, even if he suggested anything so reasonable to Mr. Stoneham, the chap would never take his advice.

He got rid of him at last, signed and stamped a few letters, and heard a church clock strike six. He wandered across to the window. Everyone else in the building had departed by now, clock-watchers to a man, he reflected. But though there was still a certain amount of activity in the streets, none of it appeared to be centred on this office. A few late workers hurried towards the mouth of the tube station, others made for the nearest bus-stop. An occasional car ran past, someone paused at the corner to post a letter. Crook reminded himself that a watched pot never boils and came back to his desk to make out a receipt for Gordon to sign. " I, Alistair Gordon, Esq., of 30 Nash Square, N.W. hereby acknowledge . . . etc., etc." and to dot the i's and cross the t's careful Mr. Crook pasted a picture of the wallet to the sheet.

At half past six he telephoned Gordon's office, and a charwoman's voice told him they'd all gone home before she and her colleagues arrived. Crook waited a little longer and then rang the house in Nash Place, but he could hear the bell shrilling away into nothingness and replaced the receiver. A quarter of an hour later he put the wallet into a plain envelope, shoved it in his pocket and prepared to call it a day. He threw the receipt into a drawer. He wouldn't be needing it now, but it would do for his file of curiosities when the case was closed. Every fibre in him revolted against the notion of walking mildly into the police station and making them a present of all he knew, but no one was getting much fun out of this. He didn't suppose Sid Bent was going to care for what the police would say to him. Sam Barnard was like young Holland, he wouldn't give a row of pins for anyone's opinion.

The telephone shrilled as he reached the door, and he dashed at it, thinking it must be his man at last, but no one answered when he yanked off the receiver, all he got was the dialling tone. Putting it back he remained, like the famous uffish man, a while in thought. Then he dialled Gordon's home number again with the same result. So whoever it was who had cut off so abruptly, the call hadn't been made from the house in Nash Place. Crook pressed his hard brown hat over his ears and left the office. It was a new hat and of a still fierier brown than its predecessor. When he'd got it in place he could have walked straight on to the stage of the Victoria Palace.

The one waiting by the pay phone in the hall heard the door close and the key turn. Then a light flashed on the top floor, the steps came down. Crook was wondering about Gordon, if he had intended to come, if he'd gone to the police on his own account, only in that case why hadn't they contacted their arch-enemy, A. C. ? Or had his lawyer told him, if he wanted to prove his manhood, to tangle with a cobra, or try playing tig with a charging rhino, but at all costs leave Crook alone? The last light didn't come on when he pressed the switch, but the front door of the building was on a line with the staircase, and anyway, wasn't he Arthur Crook, who could see in the dark? He was half-way down the last flight when something, delicate as a feather, stirred in his brain. He could have sworn he heard a movement, stealthy as a cat, but whether above or below he couldn't be certain. He put his hand in his pocket for the torch he always carried, not stopping, because a moving object is a more difficult target, and he felt the thing cut him sharply across the knees, the oldest booby-trap of all, a string or a piece of wire fastened across the stairs. He hadn't got a chance, one hand fumbling in his pocket, the other out-thrown for some support that wasn't there. Down he came, solid as a stone to the stone floor below. Thereafter he knew nothing but a brief spasm of a pain that was like a rock splitting his head open. Even without the fall it would have sent him careering into the dark. And the surprise that he should be so easily hoodwinked was momentarily greater than the pain. He thought he smelled blood but before he could be sure of that the darkness seemed to collect itself into an immense crashing fist that fell on him like a boulder. Thereafter he knew no more what was happening around him than in the hour before his birth.

CHAPTER XI

AFTER RUPERT HAD hastened back to his father's office, planning a lie that might hold water, to account for his long absence, Juliet travelled to the Brigade headquarters in Rumbold Street. Her rehearsal had ended at midday. Three of the cast were in a live broadcast that afternoon—" These planners, darling," they said, " simply arrange it to see how much we can endure. The Russians could learn a lot from them." Now Paul had gone the office had to be shut for long periods. Colin and Evelyn had been in favour of closing it altogether, but the two girls wouldn't hear of it. When Torquil came back he'd be horrified. . . . To-day she was thankful for a quiet place where she could sit and consider. She rang up the other Brigadiers, leaving messages where she couldn't get the principals. Urgent meeting at the Duck and Daisy 8.30 she said. She did two or three other calls, glad there was no curious old cat half-opening the door of her bed-sitter in the hopes of hearing something spicy on the public phone. A few people dropped in for literature and any gossip there might be going, only they were unlucky, and about 4.30 a cub reporter popped his impudent nose round the door and asked if there'd been any developments.

"You should get after that Mr. Crook," he said. "Doesn't he know he's a public entertainer?"

Julie surprised herself as much as the young man when she picked up a telephone directory and heaved it at him.

"Call yourself the Peace Brigade," said the young man indignantly. "Someone should buy you a dictionary."

At 7 o'clock she closed the office. No one had come in for more than half an hour and it wasn't likely there'd be anyone else now. The sales had started up west and it was the late shopping night. She drifted into the Duck and Daisy on the chance that one of the others, unable to rest, had come, too, but there were only two or three rather sullen-looking drinkers being served by Sally. Julie perched herself on a stool at the end of the bar that advertised Snacks always Available, and ordered Scotch eggs and asked if she could have coffee.

"I'll make you a cup of Instant, dear," said kind-hearted Sally. "Mr. Prentiss doesn't really like it, but seeing he's not around . . ." She looked over her shoulder, as if she expected him to materialise like the Demon King. "On your owney-oh?" she said, bringing the coffee.

"The others'll be along. We're expecting Mr. Crook later."

And none too soon, Sally thought. A girl like that, with

her career depending so much on her looks, shouldn't be going round with that haggard air. A voice was raised in the Private Bar and she hurried off. Julie picked desultorily at the eggs and thought of smoked salmon and champagne.

At about 8 o'clock the others started to drift in, all except Jos Wymark.

"I couldn't get him to speak to," Julie admitted. "His secretary, a haughty piece, said she hadn't the least idea-r when he'd be in but she'd pass the message on. Of course, she couldn't say if he'd be free. Would he know who the message came from?"

"Oh well, warning to all girls, never marry a doctor, he's in and out like a wireworm through a three-pronged fork, never there when expected, but turning up when his presence could well be dispensed with."

Rupert came later than the rest. "My old man," he exploded. "I'll swear if they cut him open they'd find a time machine instead of a heart. Tore me off a strip in front of about half the office for overstaying my leave, he called it, how pompous can you get? And made me stop on and finish some chore. . . . His proper place is Dotheboys Hall. And yet if I were to push him downstairs they'd call it murder."

"So would everyone else," said Colin sensibly. "Do belt up. One thing, you're not likely to get snared by some designing female like Eve and me. Any girl's going to think twice before saddling herself with that kind of father-in-law."

Rupert turned towards the bar. "Whisky-and-soda, Jim. I need it to settle my nerves."

"I'll bring it, Mr. Bowen," offered Jim obligingly. When he came over an instant later he said, "We've been so busy this evening I hadn't realised you were all here. I've got a message from Mr. Crook. . . ." Rupert almost dropped his glass.

"What's that you said?"

"I understood you were expecting him, but something's come up, and he won't be able to make it. But if he can he'll look in at the Casbah later."

" Is that all he said ? "

" I don't know that it was him speaking. An official sort of voice . . . I'm wanted at the bar," he added, as one or two impatient customers started ringing their tankards on the wood.

" Who'd like to bet he's still at the station ? " offered Colin. " Being held for suppression of evidence or something ? Well, that's what Rupert makes it sound like. And you must admit, the old boy sails pretty close to the wind. Still, not to worry, he's got an asbestos skin."

" I wouldn't have thought that was particularly valuable to a sailor."

" When did he ring up ? " Julie wondered. " All right, I'll ask Jim. I want a refill anyway."

Business was brisk, and Sally was momentarily in the other bar. She waited a minute while Jim pulled beer handles and jerked the tops off bottles and measured out toy doses of spirit to the accompaniment of a certain amount of chaff.

"I can make it a double if you say so, sir," was Jim's persistent sedate retort.

A dubious-looking character with a crust of greyish beard pressed a bit closer.

" Busy to-night ? " he offered. Julie paid no attention.

Jim came over. " Another half, Jim," she said. " What time did the message come through ? "

Jim thought. " I suppose about seven or thereabouts. I took it on the private line."

" Did he sound as if—as if—well, never mind. Perhaps he'll turn up at the Casbah."

" I dare say." Jim made change for a chap buying gin and lime for a couple of tarty-looking girls, who'd somehow got into his place and were wondering if they'd mistaken the entrance to the communal cemetery. " Yes, sir ? " To Crustybeard. " What for you ? "

Crustybeard smiled. " I was just thinking—if this lady's been disappointed, well, I'm at a loose end myself this evening. . . ."

Julie gave him a shove that pushed him against a man

farther along the bar and about eighteen-pennyworth of whisky transferred itself to the holder's suit. Julie left them arguing. " I'm getting violent," she said in desolate tones, when she rejoined the group. " I tried to brain a reporter this afternoon and I've just given someone what Mr. Crook would call a poke in the bread-basket. . . ."

" Good for you," said Ruth. " Don't you hate the way they all gloat ? "

There was an air of nervousness about all of them to-night, as if they sensed some crisis close at hand.

: :   : :

The policeman on the beat walked twice past Crook's office, noting that the old glutton for work was making a night of it. The Old Superb stood like a faithful steed outside the building, and the constable reflected that, if a new client surfaced even at this hour, he'd find Crook ready and waiting. It was shortly before 11 p.m. when he passed the office for the first time and nearly half past when he came back. And now something seemed to him to be wrong. Glancing upwards, he saw there was no light in the old buzzard's window, and though he waited to see the landing lights spring up to guide the lawyer downwards, the house stayed dark as a grave. He saw, too, that the street door hadn't been fastened, so he pushed it open, and pressed the light switch. And nothing happened, so he brought his bull's-eye lantern into play and what he saw sent him flying to the pay phone in the corner. As a rule the news that an elderly chap had taken a purler at this time of night wouldn't have aroused any special interest, had one or two and missed his footing, naughty old man and why wasn't he at home anyway ? But this was Arthur Crook, and the word went out for an ambulance toot sweet.

Two more officers, an inspector called Fieldfare and a sergeant, named Buck, arrived before the ambulance did. The police constable looked surprised. A simple case of accident. . . .

" Accident my foot," snorted Fieldfare. " Crook doesn't have accidents like that. Besides, isn't he the chap who can see in the dark ? "

And an instant later, kneeling beside the recumbent man. he added, " If any Harley Street wallah can explain to me how a man can fall on his big fat puss and simultaneously smash in the back of his head, I'll apply for my pension. No, someone had it in for him, and, for once, they caught him on the hop."

He looked up. " That electric light bulb, the light that failed," he observed. " Take a look, Harris." (Harris was the police constable.) And when Harris went gingerly up the stairs, because he could reach the swinging flex over the banisters, he gave the bulb a twist and the light flashed on.

" Fancy the old fox being caught out so easy," Fieldfare began, and then Harris said: " There's something here you should see, sir," and he indicated a mark on the banister where the paint had been newly scraped. Fieldfare looked at once at the wainscot opposite the rail, and there it was, a small newly-drilled hole in the woodwork.

" So that's how it was done. Bit of rope, bit of wire, and Bob's your uncle. Where's that flaming ambulance ? "

At the door the sergeant was speaking to a man who seemed to have materialised out of the night.

" This office is closed, sir," he was saying firmly.

" They're speaking of an accident," the new-comer explained. He was a powerfully-built dark-haired man, who looked as if he could take on half a dozen policemen before breakfast. " I'm a doctor." He produced a card. Dr. Jocelyn Wymark. " I was coming back from the Bloomsbury Clinic—I've got a private patient there and he took a turn for the worse this evening and they sent for me—and I heard talk of an accident. I thought . . ."

Fieldfare came down to the doorway and peered out. Like the rats who sprang from every nook and cranny to follow Hamelin's Pied Piper, a host of shadowy forms had assembled. At sight of the inspector one of them shouted to know what had happened.

" There's been an accident," the inspector shouted back. " Nothing for any of you to do. Go home."

" Is it Mr. Crook ? " inquired another voice.

As if they didn't know! Who else would be working in the office at this hour of night?

"Where do they come from?" muttered Buck irritably, as though they were an army of bugs jumping out of a wainscot and that was more or less how he thought of them. "Everything's under control," he told them.

In the hall Wymark was saying, "This man's been coshed. Do you know who he is?"

He was startled when the sergeant emitted a sound like the bark of the fox.

"Well, at least there's one man doesn't know Mr. Crook," he ejaculated.

The new-comer's response was just as surprising. "Arthur Crook? Well, whaddyou know? Case of the biter bit. Nothing to be done till we get him to hospital."

The inspector came back. "Turn down your set," he growled. "Once that mob realises there's been foul play they'll come swarming in like rats. How he does it, swelp me, I don't know, but the D.P.P. and the Chief Commissioner of Scotland Yard could both be knifed and they wouldn't turn over in bed, but tell them someone's made a murderous attack on old Uncle Arthur and there'll be no holding 'em." He supposed somehow the rumour had gone round the adjacent residential squares and alleys, possibly the old man himself sending out thought waves, he wouldn't put anything past Crook. "Next thing you know they'll fire the local nick," he added gloomily. But then wheels sounded outside and the blessed ambulance rolled up.

Just as moths are reputed to be able to summon their appointed mates from the next village simply by waggling their antennæ, so the original spectators seemed to be sending out their individual thought-waves, because a night-lorry turned off the main road and the driver leaned out of his cab to know what was up. When about fourteen voices enlightened him he said, "Lumme, they'll be dropping that bomb next." And then, "Have they got the chap who did it? They'd best get a move on or they'll find themselves alongside him in the ambulance."

It was instructive that it never occurred to any of them to believe the police version of an accident.

: : : :

After the ambulance had driven off, the police opened up Crook's office with the key they found in his pocket, and started going through it with a tooth-comb. The place looked chaotic, it was only when they came to examine it more closely that they realised nothing was really out of place. It was just that he kept his files in somewhat unconventional places. And so they found the receipt Crook had made out for his visitor to sign, and on an engagement pad on his desk, written in Crook's best hieroglyphics, they made out two names. 5. o'clock. Stoneham. 6. Gordon.

"Fun and games with a wallet," observed Fieldfare. "Point is, where is it?"

There was no sign of a wallet in the office, and the hospital, questioned, reported a shabby purse affair found in the pocket of the injured man, but the police didn't suppose that was the one Crook had had in mind.

"Best get in touch with this Mr. Alistair Gordon," remarked the inspector gloomily. He looked at his watch. "No reason why we should be the only ones who don't get a fair night's sleep. Though if Crook snuffs it, a jury 'ud be justified in bringing a verdict of suicide. Who does the fellow think he is? He knew he was up against a killer. . . ."

But no one bothered to answer that question, because they all knew. Crook thought of himself as the chap who could always go one better than the police.

: : : :

The Gordons had one of those charming Nash houses in Regent's Park for which Fiona's father had paid £25,000. When their front-door bell rang in the small, the very small, hours of the morning, they thought at first it was drunks coming to the wrong door.

"They'll go away," said Fiona grandly.

Only they didn't.

Alistair got reluctantly out of bed and peered through the curtains. There was a car outside, and his heart missed a beat when he realised the driver was a policeman.

" Police ? " said Fiona incredulously. " What on earth's been going on ? You'd better open the door. Perhaps there's been an accident and they want to borrow a telephone."

" I thought they always worked on a walkie-talkie system," her husband muttered.

" Well, let them in. We shall have the whole neighbourhood thinking we've committed a murder or something."

" Accident—murder—what a melodramatic mind you have. Probably they've just come to the wrong address."

But, of course, he didn't believe that. Some things are too good to be true.

" I'm sorry to disturb you at this hour, sir," Fieldfare told him. " We're inquiring into a case of assault."

" And you suppose I can help you ? What an extraordinary idea ! Why on earth . . . ?"

" The man in question is Mr. Arthur Crook."

Automatically he put out a hand and grabbed the nearest chair.

" What's happened to him ? "

" He was found unconscious in the hall of his office block. Perhaps we might go into one of your rooms."

Gordon jerked his head slightly, and Buck followed him in.

" Yes, of course. Just let me warn my wife. . . ."

But that proved unnecessary, for at that moment Fiona appeared.

" Has everyone gone mad ? " she demanded. " Knocking us up at this time of night."

" A man's been knocked down and severely injured," the inspector told her.

" And you've made up your mind my husband's responsible ? Why ? "

" Do keep out of this, Fiona," Alistair groaned. " I don't know myself why they're here. . . ."

" We understand you had an appointment with Mr. Crook at six o'clock this evening."

" So that's why you were late ? " snapped Fiona. " All this talk about going to the pictures. . . ."

" Fiona, will you please keep out of this ? My wife can

be of no assistance, Inspector, she knows nothing of the affair. And in any case I didn't keep the appointment."

"That being so," suggested Fieldfare smoothly, "there's no need for us to detain Mrs. Gordon."

He waited while the sergeant persuaded the lady to withdraw.

"I have a right," Fiona stormed. "If you're trying to frame my husband. . . ."

"That's a serious charge to make, madam, in front of a witness. Sergeant, open the door, Mrs. Gordon isn't staying."

At any other time Alistair might have enjoyed the scene. Fiona had been calling the tune ever since that unforgettable day when she said "I will" in a fashionable West End church.

"Now, sir," Fieldfare coaxed him, as Buck came back to the room. "We'd like you to answer a few questions, but of course we can't compel you. It's up to you. If you want to contact your solicitor . . ."

"What on earth do I want with a solicitor at this stage? I've nothing to hide—that is, I don't know anything about an assault on Crook, and why you should pick on me I can't imagine. I'm only surprised no one's tried to knife him before this."

"So you do know him?"

"I met him for the first time yesterday, when he came to my office. It's true I had an appointment with him at six o'clock, but he postponed it, said something else had come up and he'd be in touch to-day." He glanced at his handsome wrist-watch. The time was almost one a.m. "How serious is it?"

"We'll know about that later on. Why were you going to see him, sir?"

"Private business," snapped Alistair.

"In connection with a wallet?"

The hunted man shot his companion a tormented glance. "Is that what he told you?"

"He hasn't been able to make a statement yet."

"Then how . . .?"

" About this wallet, Mr. Gordon. It was yours ? "

He drew a sigh that would almost have floated a boat, if a boat had happened to be handy.

" Yes. At least, I'd reason to think it was."

" Surely you'd recognise your own wallet ? "

" I hadn't actually seen it."

" No ? I thought you said he called at your office."

" He did."

" Without bringing the wallet ? "

" I was to collect it at six o'clock. Then, as I say, he cancelled the appointment."

" Ah yes. What time was this ? "

Gordon considered. " My secretary had gone home. She usually goes at five, but she'd gone a little earlier than usual, because she had an appointment with her dentist. The telephonist puts a line through to my office when she goes at five, if I'm staying on, that is, as I frequently do."

" And she had done that last night ? "

" Yes. As I wasn't meeting Crook till six I thought I might as well finish off one or two matters while the place was quiet. The cleaners come in at six, and I'm always gone before then. I suppose it was about twenty minutes later when Crook rang through. He seemed in an almighty hurry."

" Running it pretty fine, wasn't he ? "

" It wouldn't take more than twenty minutes to get to his office in a taxi—I don't bring my car into the city as a rule—I'd planned to leave about a quarter-to."

" So, when he cancelled the appointment—what did you do then ? "

" I finished the particular job I was on, and left the office. That would be about the time I'd intended to leave."

" Five forty-five ? "

" Roughly—yes."

" And—your wife said something about the pictures ? "

" I went into The Happy Mermaid and had a drink—two drinks, I believe—then I remembered my wife was sitting on a committee last night, and I didn't particularly fancy coming back to an empty flat, so I dropped into a news-reel."

(What these chaps did before there were news-reels is anyone's guess, Fieldfare observed later to Sergeant Buck.

Perhaps they told the truth, hazarded the sergeant.

You want to watch yourself, or you'll be back on the beat, Fieldfare warned him. Told the truth indeed! He grinned. Not likely we'd believe them anyway.

But that was later.)

"I see, sir. Which one was that?"

"The Recorder in Aleppo Street. Place was full of chaps filling in an hour or getting forty winks. It always is. Cheaper than a pub and . . . I got back about seven—seven-fifteen say, and found my wife had managed to cut her committee short. What time was this attack on Crook?"

"Well, seeing he's in no position to make a statement, we don't really know," Fieldfare told him. "About this wallet—it must have been pretty important."

Gordon didn't reply at once; he was thinking harder than he'd done for a long time. Say Crook didn't come round, after all, and surely it was time he took some step to oblige the multitude of chaps who'd cause to dislike him—mightn't silence once again prove golden?

"We have a picture of it," Fieldfare observed, and he groaned.

"That's probably the one Mr. Crook showed me. He asked me if I could identify it and I agreed it looked like one I'd lost. There was an initial on the corner and his description of it tallied."

"I'm still in the dark," Fieldfare confessed. "Why was this wallet so important? Why didn't he bring it round with him when he came?"

"You must know the man, never does the obvious thing."

"Did he explain how it came into his possession? And were there no documents in it when it was found?"

"I lost it in a night-club," said Alistair desperately.

Fieldfare began to see light, but what that light revealed didn't please him much.

"Does Mrs. Gordon know it's missing?"

" I've not spoken of it—she gave it to me, and you know how sentimental women are. It was a tenth wedding anniversary present, and she had it made for me specially."

And you don't want her to know where you lost it, Fieldfare reflected. Well, fair enough. But it still foxed him where Crook came in. It seemed obvious that the wallet had been used for bargaining purposes, and somehow that didn't sound like Crook's cup of tea. He was a thorn in the official side all right, but he'd always set his big puss against blackmail in all its forms, and this sounded perilously like blackmail.

" That's all I can tell you," announced Gordon abruptly. " You'll have to wait for the rest of the story till Crook comes round. If he doesn't (and what right had he to defy all the laws of nature ?) it'll be another unsolved mystery, won't it ? "

" Oh, I wouldn't say that, sir. Mr. Crook has a partner. . . ."

Gordon started. He'd forgotten all about Parsons. " Well, if you've seen him. . . ."

" Not yet. It seems he was called out of London unexpectedly yesterday midday, and so far we haven't traced him. But he'll be back, and it's not likely Mr. Crook won't have taken him into his confidence. Tweedledee and Tweedledum, that's them."

" Look here," exploded Gordon, " you can't fasten this on to me. I know nothing about it."

" You know more than you're telling, though, and we shall find it out, only if we have to do it the hard way, well, it might give us ideas."

So he told them—about the bloodstained coat and the taxi and the body in the kiosk.

" But don't think you can hang that round my neck," he shouted, and Fiona, burning with curiosity, came softly down the passage. " I never even saw his face." His own now was a horrid lardy white.

" Surely, Mr. Gordon, you must have realised it was your duty to go to the police ? "

" Why should I ? " he demanded like a defiant schoolboy.

" I couldn't tell them anything, I don't know who did it, for all I know it was this man you've arrested. After all, you must have had pretty good reason. And only a fool wants to get entangled with a murder."

" And a bigger fool who, finding himself entangled, keeps his mouth shut. You must have appreciated that this coat was one of the chief pieces of evidence. I can't promise no charge will be made," he added abruptly. " Now, had you mentioned this appointment to anyone at all ? "

" No."

" So, naturally, you hadn't mentioned its cancellation."

" There wasn't anyone to mention it to."

" You didn't happen to observe to your wife that you'd been hanging about for a man who didn't keep his appointment ? "

" I told her I'd been to the pictures." He lifted his head. " Inspector, how about this wallet ? It doesn't really play any part in the murder of this Luzky fellow. Can't you give it back to me ? "

" Oh, we couldn't do that, sir. You see, we haven't got it. Whoever knocked Mr. Crook out must have taken it with him when he scarpered. And just for the record I have to ask you—is that wallet now in your possession ? "

" Of course not. How could it be ? I tell you I didn't see Crook last night. He rang up and postponed our meeting. Oh God, I'll have a gramophone record made of the statement. . . ."

" And this was about 5.20 ? That might help, Mr. Gordon, because we know the address of his five o'clock appointment, and he might be able to tell us what time he left the office, and if Mr. Crook made a call while he himself was there."

" It could have been a little after 5.20. I didn't make a special note. I told you, I hadn't intended to leave till 5.45."

" This gentleman may have been the reason for the cancellation, if it was something very urgent—there's no correspondence so it looks as though it might have been a snap appointment. I'll have to ask you to come along to the station later—my sergeant will accompany you—to identify the coat. . . ."

"There's no need to have a policeman hanging round the house," Gordon protested. "I'm not going to do a moonshine flit."

"I'm thinking of your own safety, sir. It's not likely we can keep this information about Mr. Crook out of the papers, and if your name should get mentioned you might be quite glad to have a representative of the law on the premises, so to speak."

"You talk as if you expected me to be lynched," exclaimed Gordon, with a forced laugh.

"From our point of view, it would cause less trouble if you'd tried to knock off the Prime Minister—not speaking personally, you understand—but there won't be enough police in the Metropolitan area to save the man who did this from—well, being lynched like you suggested."

"Oh, nonsense," said Gordon uneasily. "People don't get lynched over here."

"There has to be a first time for everything. And Mr. Crook's bodyguard, as you might call them, are never what you'd call conspicuous for law and order."

"I'd like to call my solicitor," said Gordon sharply. "I've no statement to make till I've seen him. And Crook himself can alibi me for the kiosk murder. He said as much himself."

"Then we must hope he comes round quickly, mustn't we, sir?"

Gordon found he was trembling in his shoes. How could he, how could any man, guess what he was letting himself in for when he went along to have a little fun and refreshment at the Fiddlers' Rest? Fifteen minutes after Fieldfare had departed he was wishing fervently he'd accompanied him. A cell would be heaven compared with 30 Nash Square with Fiona lashing about the place like an enraged crocodile.

The morning papers carried the news. All except the starchy kind read by the B.P. (Best People) carried it on the front page. The other B.P. (Brit. Pub.) revelled in it, a number of chaps who didn't love the police as much as brothers should were frankly taken aback by the information, among them Mr. Henry Morgan, on whose behalf Crook had already swung a pretty hefty line but who was aware he wasn't out of the wood yet.

" I hope they get the bastard that did this," flamed Mr. Morgan. And quite a lot of other chaps who didn't always see eye to eye with the law spoke darkly about doing working men out of their rights. If chaps wanted to knock other chaps on the head what was wrong with M.P.s or even local councillors ? But there it was, they confided each to each. If they wanted to knock off anyone it was always the friend of the working man. And chaps who think that life on the windy side of the law is a cushy existence just don't know their onions.

The B.B.C. even gave Crook a line in the early morning news. Bill Parsons heard it at Guildford, and was out of bed like a tiger and came racing up to London in his little knockabout car at such a speed that one petrified pedestrian swore a red light turned green with terror as he approached. Knowing the metropolis like the back of his hand, he knew exactly which hospital they would have taken Crook to, and he came breezing up much too early for the authorities.

Before he stormed that fortress he slammed into a telephone box conveniently sited just opposite the hospital and rang up Wallace of the *Record.* No one, he and Crook agreed, could ever quite replace Cummings but Wallace made a pretty fair job of it.

" Waiting to see Crook," he explained. " Anything new ? "

" They're not telling us. No statement. That's all we get. You'll want your invisible cloak to get through there. The only other address in London where there's an even comparable crush is our Mr. Gordon's house in Regent's Park."

" I'll have a word with Mr. Gay Gordon myself later," promised Bill.

" Not much of the Gay about it from all accounts. The Press, amply supported by chaps who're looking to your buddy to keep them on the right side of a prison cell, are doing a little demonstratin' there. Like a trail of ants to the marmalade-pot, that's how it is. From the gate to the front door, and I dare say by now a few of them have got through the windows. There's a rumour Mrs. G. has asked for police protection."

" And, brother, is she going to need it, if anything happens to Crook," said Bill.

There wasn't a great deal of him—Crook sometimes said he looked like a tall glass of water—but he stormed the hospital like a veritable Goliath.

" 'Ere, you can't come in yet. It's not visiting hours for ages," the porter protested.

" Just heard about Mr. Crook," Bill explained.

" Must have had a nice sleep," said the porter kindly. " They've been queueing here since 6 a.m. Chaps stopping on their way to work, mark you, to ask how he is. You'd think he was Royalty."

" Royalty," explained Bill with unusual loquacity, " is an accident of birth. Crook is an Act of God."

" If you say so. But you can't go in."

" How is he ? "

" 'Olding 'is own. 'Ere, I said . . ."

" Next of kin," explained Bill.

The porter looked sceptical. " Relative ? "

" That's right. Half-brother."

The porter shrugged, let him go. Let them slap him down when he got inside.

Inside they protested at the unreasonableness of the visiting times, but Bill had neither time nor inclination for this kind of kerfuffle.

" Where is he ? " he demanded. " I want to see him. Don't tell me I shall wake the rest of the ward, because everyone knows you get your patients up with the dicky-birds."

He had approached a nurse, the first person he saw ; she looked like a human being, but it turned out she was made of basalt or something.

" Mr. Crook is very gravely ill," she said icily. " There

can be no question of his having visitors. Not that it would be any good in any case. He's unconscious."

"That being so, I can't do him any harm, can I?" said Bill. "All the same, if I can't see him I'll just hang around."

"You can't wait here," said the nurse.

"I thought a man who was dangerously ill was on open order. Which ward's he in?"

"Mr. Crook is in a private room...." She saw a doctor come hurrying through the corridor.

"Dr. Phelps," she said. "This is Mr. Crook's next of kin...." Bill was surprised to realise he'd even made that point.

"If you're as tough as he is you're not going to give the profession much work," said the doctor, and the nurse's eyes nearly turned inwards. "All right, Nurse, I'll cope," he went on. "If you've come for news all I can tell you is that a chap who could still be alive after such a fall and such a blow—I don't know what was used but it was pretty lethal—might even recover. Do they know who did it?" he inquired.

"They haven't told me," said Bill. It seemed to occur to him for the first time that the police might be interested to see him.

When he had got the latest report on Crook and been allowed to see him—and if he hadn't been exactly a beauty competition entrant before, even his own mother would have scratched him now—he went along and had a shave and some breakfast and drove down to the police station. He didn't know exactly what Crook had been cooking up, but the baby had been passed to him, and he didn't believe in any fads like swaddling clothes or veils to protect a peach-like complexion. In short, he told them everything he knew.

"If the wallet isn't on the premises X must have taken it with him," said the police inspector. "And there can't be more than one man primarily interested in that."

"Whom had you in mind?" asked Bill, and his companion goggled.

"Who do you suppose?"

"You can't mean you're pinning this on Gordon?" exclaimed Bill. "I know he wanted Crook's blood, but it doesn't make sense that he should be responsible for this." And he told them why.

: : : :

For three days everyone waited. Crook struggled back to consciousness, recognised Bill, unfortunately caught sight of a policeman's uniform, and faded out again.

"He may never remember, Mr. Parsons," Sister said.

"Don't you believe it," said Bill. "He'll come round suddenly, and that's when you want to watch out. He'll go through the ceiling when you're not noticing. You've got a tiger on your hands there, Sister, and don't forget it."

The police were busy enough. They put Joe Francis through the mangle, gave Sid Bent whatfor and asked a blandly smiling Sam Barnard if he realised that withholding essential evidence concerning a crime is an indictable offence. They found Crook's unexpected five o'clock visitor, who assured them that he (Crook) had put through no calls between 5 o'clock and, say, 5.40. Gordon stuck to his story that he'd left his office at 5.45 and gone straight to The Mermaid.

There was no trace of the wallet, though rubbish dumps and dustbins and public vehicles and any place where a man could have dropped it were searched. The most sensible place to put it would probably be the river, and if it was there it might not be dredged up till that day when the sea (and all smaller waters) give up the dead that are in them.

The police, treating Crook with more respect than usual, were more inventive than he'd ever known them. They were having a busy time, with a constant watch on Gordon's house, for Gordon's own protection.

"Save a lot of trouble if we pulled him in," Oakapple acknowledged. "But Parsons made a point, and we don't want to arrest a second man we may have subsequently to release."

And there was still no sign of the Hunter jewels.

"If they or the wallet or some foolproof evidence doesn't surface in the next forty-eight hours we shall have Parsons doing one of his famous cat acts and coming over the roofs and down the chimney," prophesied the superintendent gloomily. "You don't remember him, any of you lot, but—well, when he joined up with Crook the general impression was that the pair of them could have taken on the Big Five—and if any of you quote me, I'll swear you're all as drunk as lords. Bill worked on his own and he never used violence. They don't come like that any more." He sounded positively wistful. The next instant he sighed. "How old is he now? We ought to be able to tell."

"Round about fifty?" someone hazarded.

"And then some. And Crook, I understand, is a perennial fifty-five. So that gives us another twenty years of the pair, say, seeing the stamina they've both got. Roll on, retirement."

He'd been heard to observe that chaps like these were more trouble than all the criminal classes. It was like being given a book of the rules to read in Chinese and getting strafed by the boss because you couldn't make head or tail of it.

CHAPTER XII

IT WOULD BE HARD to say who was the more pleased when Crook decided to discharge himself from hospital, the patient himself or the hospital authorities. Ward Sister had no objection to the ordinary run of V.I.P.s, but Crook's kind were nothing but a cracking nuisance. For one thing, his well-wishers had no sense of discipline, imagined they could come drifting along at any old hour and as many as they pleased. "Two at a time at 2 p.m.," they chanted derisively, when the hospital's rules were pointed out to them. "What a liberty! We got to work, see?"

"Really, they are the most extraordinary crowd. I find myself counting the beds after they've gone," Sister confided to a colleague. "Work for them must be like living in a perpetual shady nook."

It was a pity she didn't say as much to Crook; he'd have appreciated it.

He had his point of view, too. "Talk about taking your life in your hands," he assured Bill. "Every time the door opens and a dirty great rozzer comes in, what guarantee have I he didn't hire the gear from Mossbros and hasn't got a flick knife clutched in his dimpled fist?"

The Brigadiers had come singly and in pairs but they got no satisfaction from their man.

"I'm on sick pay," Crook pointed out. "I can't tell the police anything, so how can I tell you? Just wait till I'm on my feet, though, and that'll need to be soon unless I'm to leave here in a box."

On the day he decided his nerves wouldn't stand the strain any longer he sent a message to Jocelyn Wymark.

"Open order," he said, "and, seeing you're like me and work all round the clock, you'll find time to drop by."

And when Jos came in he said sunnily, "I don't think I've had the pleasure to date. That is, I was *non compos* the last time, and the time before—the night we might have met—you were in the Midlands, so I'm told."

Jos caught on quite quickly. "The night Paul was eliminated—that's true. Arranging an exhibition for the town council. A photographic unit was lending us their records and the public reacts to pictures better than anything else. You can shut up a book or switch off a programme, but there's something compulsive about a collection of photographs."

Crook thought, "Another eager beaver. We'll be back to Hiroshima in a minute." And so they were, but not for long.

"What can I do for you?" Jos inquired, and Crook asked him: "Got any time off between now and midnight? I'm pulling out, see. Bill's coming round with the Superb, and he can make it any time you say."

"*I* say? I'm not your medical attendant, Mr. Crook."

"I wouldn't be talking to you this way if you were. No, the idea is to get clear without giving X a chance to plug me again. You'd be surprised how easy it is to stick a knife in a chap in a crowd—or maybe you wouldn't. So I thought—say Bill waits outside the front of the hospital with the Superb, sort of trade mark, see, the grateful authorities might connive at me sneaking out, alley-cat-wise, by the back."

"Where I'm waiting with my car? I should think they'd co-operate to the hilt. You've been quite an embarrassment to them, Mr. Crook."

"Go on," said Crook resignedly. "Tell me it's all my fault some chap tried to crack my skull. Must have been a stranger or he'd have known he was wasting his time. Only goes to show it sometimes pays to be a square. Nowadays I'm told the nobs only wear hats to weddings and funerals, but I tell you, if I hadn't been wearing my titfer that night, the hospital would have been spared their blessed embarrassment. I mean, they'd have been able to cart me along straight to the mortuary."

He reached out and opened a little locker beside his bed. From it he took a weird and awesome object that the doctor didn't at first identify as a hat.

"Is that it?" he murmured.

Crook looked at it affectionately. "Such a pot should have such a lid," he quoted. "Mind you, it's like me, it's seen better days, but then it's not as young as it was, either. And when I have a hat I expect it to work for me. None of these airy fairy Lilian effects perched on the top of your skull ready to be snatched off at a moment's notice. Mine fits well over the ears—well, I've only got two and they're important to me."

"Sort of crash helmet," suggested Jos, regarding the object with a kind of horrid fascination.

"When X swung his little cosh what he did was to shove it farther over my skull; quite a job they had to prise it off, I'm told. Mind you, it's lost its pristine freshness, but a rose-petal's still a rose-petal, however crumpled. I shall have it put under a glass case when I get back," he added simply.

"Ever thought of donating it to the Crime Museum at the Yard?" suggested Jos, straight-faced as a drink of milk.

He agreed to come round about five o'clock as near as he could and drive Crook direct to the Brigade Headquarters.

" When the chaps find they've been diddled some of 'em will go pounding round to Brandon Street," Crook explained. " If any of 'em should tumble to my notion, well, there'll be a deputation waiting for them, and you know what peace propagandists are. Speaking personally, I'd sooner find myself up against a man-eating tiger."

The news got round like wild-fire that Crook was pulling out. Bill reinforced the rumour by appearing in the hospital forecourt at the wheel of the Superb ; he left it there and went inside. After about twenty minutes he came back, alone.

" You can put your gear away," he told the newshounds. " You won't be seeing Crook this afternoon, after all. Change of plan."

He put the Superb into gear and shot away. By the time they realised what had happened Crook was in the basement room at Battersea. The Big Five were waiting for him, and they gave him a mixed reception. They were angry—at least the girls were—because Gordon was still at liberty and Torquil wasn't.

" Your precious pal's O.K. where he is," Crook insisted. " And I dare say Gordon wouldn't mind changing places with him. At least they don't let your ever-loving accompany you to jail, and since the story's made the front pages of the gutter Press I wouldn't give the price of a pint for his chances. A case of ' O Death, where is thy sting ? ' if ever there was one."

" But he tried to murder you ! " cried Colin. " Even the police (who hate your guts, he meant) must take some notice of that."

Crook gawped at him. " Whatever gave you the idea it was Gordon ? Anyway, till he joins the Magicians' Circle it's hard to see how he could have been at work with his stonemason's hammer in Bloomsbury Street when, on his own statement, he was watching a horror film—well, contemporary news, it comes to the same thing—in the Strand."

" Who says he was at the pictures ? "

"He does."

"And you believe him?"

"He wasn't in his office, because the cleaners were there, and he wasn't at home because Mrs. G. got back earlier from her committee than she anticipated, just turned her Medusa glance on them and they all turned into stone, no one recalls seeing him lush up at a bar—he could just as easy have been at the pictures as anywhere. The place he wasn't at was 123 Bloomsbury Street."

They looked dazed. "You mean, you really had put him off?"

"I didn't have to. Someone did it for me."

"You've become very trusting all of a sudden," suggested Rupert. "What proof is there there ever was such a message?"

"That's part of the evidence I've got to collect. No, if it had been Gordon that night he wouldn't have been satisfied to take the wallet, he'd have gone upstairs and hunted up the photograph he knew I had, because I'd showed him a copy. Not much sense having the genuine article so long as I had the negative. Anyway, it was part of our agreement that he should get that when I'd got his signature."

"You didn't say anything about a photograph," said Juliet slowly.

"Didn't I, sugar? Well, you know what they say—old men forget. But you see my point about Gordon? Only had to help himself to the key in my pocket and Bob's your uncle. Only other chap who could have shed a little light was Joe Francis, and don't ask me who he was, I've got enough on my plate as it is, but take it from me he's run out of matches. Any questions?"

"Two," said Jos briskly, before anyone else could speak. "(a) What use was the wallet to anyone but Gordon, and (b) how could X be certain Gordon wouldn't have an alibi for the time you were coshed?"

"Answer No. 1 coming up—the idea in trying to douse my glim wasn't to get hold of the wallet. As you say, it wasn't much use to anyone but the original owner. But X wanted me out of the way and by removin' the wallet he was casting suspicion in Gordon's direction. If (b) Gordon had an alibi, well, that was the police's headache. They might argue he'd hired a thug. The real point at issue was that I should be stopped, permanently if possible, from getting after the real chap who did for Paul."

Jos plodded on as indomitable as the original Old Superb.

" Who else would know about the wallet—and Gordon's appointment for that evening ? "

" There," said Crook, " you have the crux of the situation. Who would ? " He looked at them as bright-eyed and heartless as a cuckoo in the nest.

" Anyone you told, I suppose," hazarded Rupert.

" That makes it a close field. I didn't even get a chance to tell Bill, not before he lighted out for Folkestone. The only couple I confided in are sitting with us now."

" You said I could tell the others, Mr. Crook," exclaimed Juliet quickly. " I called the meeting for 8.30."

" I didn't get any message," said Jos. " I was out when Julie rang, and as soon as I came in I had surgery and after surgery there was this S O S from the Bloomsbury Clinic."

" Then maybe someone mentioned it just by chance."

" But why should anyone who heard it just by chance want to do you an injury, Mr. Crook ? "

" ' And thick and fast they came at last, and more and more and more '," Crook agreed. " Not the oysters, the difficulties. No, I can't think why either."

" It was to our interest that you should stop in cracking good form," Colin protested.

" Well, clearly not everyone's," murmured Crook.

The penny that had been poised in mid-air for some minutes here fell with a clang. They sat in a dead silence as if, dropping, it had raised such a clamour, they were all deafened. It was Rupert who said, " You mean, it has to be one of our mob ? "

" You said it, not me."

" But that would mean one of us is Walter. Which is *reductio ad absurdum.*"

" Or, of course, one of you might know who Walter is.

But don't try and tell me he's a red herring, however fishy the situation may appear, because I shan't believe you."

"I don't believe it," said Ruth. "None of us would do that."

Bill broke up the assembly by appearing in the doorway to declare, "I shall get a parking ticket if I hang round much longer. Anyway, your first day out from hospital, the doc here will probably agree you've done enough."

"Possibly more than enough," Jos agreed. "In fact, it's gone through my mind we may have brought him away too soon. There are some injuries that aren't instantly apparent. . . ."

"Nuthouse?" suggested Crook. "Don't give me that. I warned you all from the start that if I undertook this case I shouldn't pull any punches. And I'm not going to strain your patience much longer, another twenty-four hours or so, and the issue should be settled one way or the other. Now, I'd be obliged if you'd all stick around in your own places to-night, I might need a bit of help. And if you'd inscribe your phone numbers . . ." He produced a little pocket-book and passed it to Colin, who sat nearest.

"What sort of help?" asked Rupert suspiciously.

"I thought you'd be ready for anything," said Crook, looking surprised. "Also, while you're about it, look after yourselves, you innocent ones. It's later than you think."

The six people he left behind heard the car drive away before any of them spoke. Then Evelyn said, "Did you ever go on one of those contraptions at a fair that whirl you heavenwards in a little car and then, without warning, turn you upside down? The only time I tried I lost everything that wasn't actually attached. Well, Crook has much the same effect on me."

"If you mean you're going to be sick the bathroom's along the passage," Jos reminded him. And he added, "I wouldn't blame you. I don't feel any too steady myself."

"If you ask me," announced Rupert jauntily, and they knew it didn't matter whether they asked or not, they were going to be told, "that scene misfired a bit. The guilty party was supposed to drop down in a faint or stagger back exclaiming, 'How did you guess? What did I do?' Instead of which reaction was practically nil."

"How do you know reaction was practically nil?" asked Jos, with no change of tone. "We don't know what kind of reaction Crook was looking for. I noticed he piled off as meek as milk when that chap, Parsons, came in, and I wouldn't say he was the type to leave before he'd got what he came for."

Crook spent the next two hours dealing with the correspondence that had been piling up in his flat during his absence. He had the enviable ability to settle, like a persistent bee, on one flower at a time, and he put the Aslett affair out of mind while he worked. He felt the new life coming back with each succeeding minute, like a balloon being gradually inflated with air.

"Air? Hydrogen," he thought, exultantly. He had almost forgotten the fascination of crime and its solution. Then he decided it was time to go along and wet his whistle, but he rang all the numbers he'd been given by the Brigadiers, using a different voice each time, and each time he got the answer that whoever it was was either on the other end of the line or at all events on the premises. So he picked up his flat brown cap—he hadn't had time to replace the treasured bowler—and called at the Duck and Daisy.

"Nice to see you back, Mr. Crook," said Jim, overdoing it a bit, Crook thought, seeing he wasn't an habitué. But the next words disillusioned him. "Perhaps the Peace lot will start coming again. Afraid of publicity perhaps, we've had the Press hanging around. I've often said I could do with a bit more publicity, but when it does come it's the wrong kind."

"Hard cheese," sympathised Crook. Assuming Jim ever made the Pearly Gates he'd be sure to have forgotten his sun-glasses and complain that the light hurt his eyes; it wouldn't be Heaven for him if there wasn't something wrong.

"They'll be back," Crook promised. "It's not as though they'd taken the pledge."

He carried off his pint to a convenient corner and sat

drinking. The Brigadiers appeared to be taking him seriously, there wasn't so much as a nose out of them until a little before ten when the door swung open violently and a man came in, looking as grey as putty, calling to Jim, "Double Scotch and you can forget the water. Mucking car accident just up the road," he added to anyone who cared to listen. "Blood all over the place."

"Till they make it clear who has the right of way at Hosegood's Corner we'll go on getting smashes," said a fearfully sober chap, who'd been putting 'em away all right and might have saved his money and drunk water out of the kitchen tap for all the effect they had on him. Jim knew how to pick 'em, thought Crook, wave your fairy wand and you'd have a first-class mortician's outfit on your hands.

"Doctor's coming along to get a drink," the gloomy one went on, "and I don't mind buying it for him."

The doctor came in a minute or two later and it was Jocelyn Wymark.

"I hope you haven't been trying to contact me," he said smoothly, coming over to Crook's side. "I got called out to a hæmorrhage, and coming back I had to run into this. You know how it is."

"There were chaps like that in the war," agreed Crook, giving him a not particularly friendly glance. "Wherever they went the bombs followed. How is he—the injured man, I mean?"

"He'll live," said Jos. "You might take a leaf out of his book."

"Meaning?"

"Whoever batted you on the head meant business."

"I don't have much to do with any other kind."

"You're fond of clichés, aren't you?" Jos went on. "There's one that says lightning never strikes twice in the same place. It's not true."

"Warning me?" murmured Crook.

"Play bridge? Poker? I thought not. The way you laid your cards out on the table this evening . . ."

"Chaps are more inclined to make a move when they know what cards you're holding. Anyway," he added casually, " the ones that matter are the ones you've got up your sleeve. How come ? " he added. " Losing your nerve ? "

" No one's after me. Still, for your own sake, I hope you're near the end. That chap come with you to-night ? "

" Chap ? "

" Your bodyguard "

" Bill ain't like me. He don't care about beer."

" I'll walk back with you," Jos offered.

" What is this ? " demanded Crook. " Do you know something I don't ? "

Jos shook his head. " Just wondering if you know enough to round off the story with the right ending."

" I had a client once," said Crook, who seldom found himself at a loss, no matter what turn the conversation might take. " Writer he was. Used to get in no end of a stew when he was getting near the last chapter. Last chapter's the worst of the lot, he'd say. And his ever-loving would follow him round with trays of coffee and sandwiches bleating with sympathy, and one afternoon he picked up the dear little sandwich knife. . . . Lucky for her plastic surgeons know their stuff, you'd hardly be able to tell now where the knife went in. Conduct unbecoming of an officer and a gentleman, I told him, and all for a book. But I've more sympathy with him now. When you do come up against a last chapter that won't jell . . ." He was frowning. He was remembering something Bill had once told him, that there were safes you could open with your eyes shut and others you could only defeat by endless patience and experiment. Somewhere, he thought, I've missed out on a clue. Criminals always come one purler and it's when they're down you can put your big heavy beetle-crusher on them. It's different for the police, of course, they're not allowed to stamp on anyone's face. Crook hoped it was allowed for in the pension.

Jos picked up his glass, then leaned over and collected Crook's.

" Same again ? " he gestured.

" Very civil of you," said Crook. He sighed. He'd

intended to go on to The Two Chairmen, where the barman, Charlie, could have made his fortune in the diplomatic service. A cut-and-come-again chap and better than the telly any day. Dr. Jos came back with the glasses.

"On the house," he said. "Jim insists."

Which meant he couldn't just drink up and vamoose, he'd have to sit around a while longer, possibly buy another pint. Jos apparently had no such scruples. He tossed off his drink, renewed his offer of an escort and was again refused, and went out. He said something about ringing the hospital to find out about the chap. And, after all, Crook only stayed a few more minutes himself. He was feeling heavy and somehow dejected, which was unusual for him. He looked round to say good-bye to someone, but Sally had her hands full at the Public Bar and Jim must have been in the Private. He wasn't used to oiling unostentatiously out of a bar, nothing seemed quite on the dotted line to-night.

His way home—he was walking, it hadn't been worth bringing the Superb—led him past the Casbah, and he peered in, saw a face he recognised and, shrugging, went on his way. A group of noisy youths and girls jeered as he went by, reminding him of the rude kids who shouted at Elijah and got themselves devoured by bears for their pains. Unfortunately no one in Earls Court kept bears.

"Go home, you naughty old man," someone called. "It's not a cat house."

On another evening he would have found the appropriate retort ready on his tongue, but to-night his attention was diverted. But the episode jarred. Old man—perhaps that was it. He'd lived for so long that living had become a habit, he couldn't conceive of himself needing the hospitality of a coffin or the services of a professional burial merchant. He was shivering a bit, there was a cold wind coming up the street to-night. And then he heard them, the sound of footsteps coming softly through the shadows. He was a vain man, boasting not only that he could see in the dark like a cat, but also that his auditory capacities equalled those of the bat, that can distinguish sounds beyond the human ear. He slowed down, wondering if the road had always seemed as long as it did to-night, and instantly the footsteps slowed also. He had no doubt now why they were there, but there was nothing to be done except emulate Felix, the cat of his youth, who kept on walking. Once he did hesitate, when he passed a corner and saw a telephone box a few steps along a side street. He took a couple of steps in the direction of the kiosk, and then saw the contemptuous notice OUT OF ORDER. It seemed obvious the angels had got tired of working on his side, and in a way you couldn't blame them. He shook himself, shaking off this unaccustomed feeling of lethargy, hurried on and then he saw something that lightened his heart. At a corner ahead were lights and some garish-looking posters and he realised he was approaching Ruth's flea-pit. He took fresh heart. Let him once conceal himself in that darkness and he might be safe. It was new to him to be the stalked rather than the stalker, but he didn't try to kid himself. He knew he was up against someone who had killed before and would quite ruthlessly kill again, and this time there'd be no mistake. The footsteps came faster, and he swerved abruptly and crossed the street. As in several of the smaller, more old-fashioned news cinemas, the box office was practically on the pavement. There was an anæmic middle-aged woman at the window, lethargically counting the evening's takings. Even in his present dazed state Crook could see that wouldn't take her long. He pulled a half-crown out of his pocket and rapped on the window. She paid no attention, went on laboriously separating the silver and coppers into small heaps. Crook rapped again, at which she straightened and shook her head. The window itself was closed and he couldn't see how it could be opened from this side. Most likely, he thought, sensibly, it couldn't. He could hear the footsteps hesitating on the other side of the street; at any instant they would start moving in his direction. He thudded on the glass with his closed fist, and suddenly she snapped the little panel open and said rudely, "You're too late. There's a notice. No admission after 10.25. We close at a quarter-to."

"Surely the management doesn't object to taking my two bob for fifteen minutes' entertainment?" Crook urged.

" If I like to chuck my money away, isn't that my funeral ? "

He heard the feet start to cross the road a little lower down.

" I told you, you're too late." As he stooped closer she took fright and uttered a sharp scream. An inner door flew open and a yellow-faced little man appeared, wearing a dingy purple uniform.

" What is it, Nellie ? "

" I'm telling him, no more admission to-night."

" It doesn't make sense," said Crook. " Anyway, I'm coming in. I'm not . . ."

" 'E's 'ad a skinful," said the little yellow man scornfully. " 'Ere, bugger off if you don't want me to call the police."

Even feeling as though he was stumbling into a dark ocean, Crook could retain a vision of a police car rolling up to take Arthur Crook away to the cells. Well, better that than Arthur Crook in his coffin.

" You do that," he said thickly, and put out his hands for support. He knew what was wrong with him now and part of his sickness stemmed from self-disgust.

" I knew it," proclaimed Nellie. " 'E's after the till. Soaked, that's what 'e is."

He didn't say any more. It was too late. The footsteps had come alongside, the hand was on his arm.

" It's all right," said the voice. " The poor chap's ill."

" If that's what you call it."

" It is what I call it." The voice sounded more severe now. " I'm a doctor. I'll look after him. You don't know who he is, I suppose ? "

They shook their heads. " Never seen 'im before."

" He's probably got some mark of identification. But he really is ill. What was the trouble ? " he added.

" Trying to get in, when there's a notice there saying patrons can't be admitted this time of the evening. We've been through all that," the man added, his little yellow rat's face working viciously. " Chaps come in last thing and they don't all come out after the Queen. Hide in the toilet, under the seats, wouldn't believe how cunning they are. We 'ad a deserter only last month, police after him, of course, in he came, how were we to know—stopped in all night and fair wrecked the place. Got out through a smashed window and my cat cut 'er paw something shocking. No thought for anyone but themselves."

"Hooliganism. Yes. A great problem. I'll get this chap home. He must have taken something. . . ."

"You best get him away quick," said the little man in alarmed tones. "Nellie and me, we don't want trouble. Mind you, I still think it's the drink. . . ."

The dark waves were very close now, they engulfed him, roaring in his ears, and someone seemed to have put out the cinema lights. But they were going to close in fifteen minutes and they didn't let anyone in. A voice said unexpectedly, "That's right. The drink. Brought it—in the drink . . ."

The arm holding him tightened, he felt himself urged up the road. "Knockout drops," he went on quite clearly. And then something about a doctor. And—"I never guessed . . .

"You'll be all right in the morning," his companion soothed him. And he said something about a horse.

"Don't want a horse," demurred Crook. His wandering and unfocused eye surveyed the street into which he was now being propelled. Normally traffic was fairly brisk at this hour, but to-night there was nothing to be seen but a small private car standing beside the kerb, occupied only by the driver, head bent over a paper. A voice in Crook's brain a long way off said, go on, give a hail, but before he could collect himself the driver suddenly put the car into gear and shot off. It was almost as though the arrival of this odd couple was a signal.

And at practically the same moment a taxi came chugging round the corner, and Crook's companion hailed it.

"What's wrong with 'im?" asked the driver, and the crisp voice said: "He's not well. I'm a doctor, I'll take responsibility." It all came out as smooth as the best cream. Then he hoisted Crook into the taxi and gave the man an address.

It wasn't No. 2 Brandon Street.

CHAPTER XIII

CROOK WOKE, opened his eyes and hurriedly shut them again. He didn't know where he was, but it didn't seem very important. What mattered most of all was the cacophony of bells ringing all about him, like finding yourself in Rome on Easter morning, he supposed, hazily. He had lain there with his eyes shut for a couple of minutes before he realised the bells were ringing in his own head. Therefore, they would presently cease. He waited and slowly the sound deadened. Cautiously he opened his eyes again. He was in bed, and there was something familiar about the walls, the scarred furniture, even the orange and green blanket that covered him.

"Hell's bells!" shouted Mr. Crook, sitting up. "I'm home."

The sudden gesture was a mistake; it was as if half a dozen pendulums suddenly started swinging again. "Thick night?" he wondered. It wasn't often he had no recollection of how he'd got into his own flat. Slowly his impressions took shape, like pictures appearing on a television screen. He remembered the nightmare walk up Marston Street, the encounter with Nellie, the following footsteps.

"A Mickey Finn!" he said aloud presently. "That's what it was. Me at my age—and he slipped me a Mickey Finn."

He remembered Jos Wymark coming across carrying two glasses. "Landlord's compliments," he'd said. "Like me to see you home?" he'd asked.

"Old fox!" muttered Crook.

He staggered up and made himself coffee, strong enough to float a hen on. When he felt better he went to look for his newspaper and post. There was something in the letter-box that hadn't been there when he went out the previous evening, and hadn't been brought by a servant of the Crown, not officially, anyway. It was a strong plain manilla envelope, carefully fastened and even stuck down with a bit of sealing-paper, it bore no address but, seeing it was in his box, it was presumably intended for him. He slit open the top of the envelope and Gordon's missing wallet slid into his hand.

Five minutes later he was talking to Bill Parsons.

" The card was in my hand all the time," he said, " only I didn't recognise it. And last night clinched it. I'm going round to see Gordon now. You might meet me there in, say, forty-five minutes. I don't imagine I'll be invited to breakfast. If he can't give me the ace we'll have to sneak one from out of our sleeves, goodness knows we've had enough practice."

: :   : :

For some reason Alistair Gordon couldn't get the thought of Crook out of his mind. He had heard of the fellow's release from hospital, and all the previous evening he had waited, nervous as a cat, for a summons. That was how he thought of it, not a call, a summons. He hated Crook as he'd never hated anyone, not even Fiona at her worst and most bossy. They were breakfasting together shortly before nine o'clock the day after Crook's peculiar encounter when the bell of the flat rang, a good hearty peal that was enough to take the skin off anyone of a sensitive disposition at this hour of the morning.

" Who on earth can that be at this time of day ? " Fiona demanded, and he heard himself say, " That'll be Crook," before he knew he was going to utter the words.

" Nonsense," said his wife vigorously. " You've got the man on the brain."

Alistair walked to the window. There, as immovable as a one-time mammoth, though a deal more graceful, sat the Old Superb.

The bell rang again.

" Do you want him to break the door down ? " inquired Fiona, freezingly.

Snatching up a piece of half-eaten toast, Alistair rushed

into the hall and flung open the door with a vigour that suggested the burghers welcoming the good news from Ghent ; and there he stood, every loathsome bulging pound of him, just as Alistair had expected.

" Good morning, good morning," Crook said in his expansive way, but Alistair got some satisfaction out of the realisation that he didn't look quite his normal bouncy self. Been on the tiles perhaps, he thought. With a lot of witches' grimalkins.

" I've got an office if you want to see me," Alistair snarled.

" Never mix your private and your public life. An excellent rule. Anyway, I've come to return your property."

And with a gesture that was meant to suggest Henry Irving he flung the wallet on to the carved hall table.

That took all the wind out of Gordon's sails. He gaped and gaped. Then he said in strangled tones, " You mean, it was a put-up job, you had it all the time. . . ."

" And, of course, I bumped myself on the head and while I was still unconscious removed the wire or whatever from the staircase. Be your age, man. One reason why I'm round bright and early is to make sure you didn't leave it on me last night."

Alistair spluttered and the breakfast-room door flashed open and out came Fiona like a lady dragon from her lair. Either she'd never been told that silence was golden or she'd come off her own gold standard *pro tem.*

" Alistair, what on earth . . . ? Who is this ? The famous Mr. Crook ? "

Crook ducked his big red head. " Got it in one. I . . ."

" I cannot understand why you should consider this a suitable hour for calling on my husband. Are you aware that it is barely nine o'clock ? " And at that instant a clock looking like a skeleton started to chime.

" In the U.S.A.," Crook assured her, " they're at their desks at 8.30, when it isn't 8." He might have added that they went one better in Brandon Street, where the shutters never went up at all.

Fiona wasn't listening, her glance had fallen on the wallet. " Where did that come from ? "

"Mr. Crook brought it."

"Acting as middle-man," Crook explained. He thought it would have been matey if they'd invited him to sit down or even have a cup of coffee, but it didn't seem to occur to either of them.

"You mean, someone left it on you?"

"That's what I mean."

"Who was it?"

"That's what your husband's going to help me to find out."

"The police," began Fiona, and Crook said: "Have a heart, lady. I had a thick night. Now, it won't take you above fifteen minutes," he added coaxingly, to an Alistair who looked like a pillar of salt. "And I'll pay for the calls—because that's all there is to it. I've brought a number of—well, telephone numbers," he waved a bit of paper at them, "and I want for you to ring up each in turn and talk on any subject you please for, say, a couple of minutes. If you recognise any of the voices don't say a word till you've done the lot. And the lady can listen in on the extension," he added handsomely.

"But what shall I be listening for?" persisted Gordon.

"One of this lot," Crook tapped the scrap of paper, "must have phoned you to postpone that appointment. Always assuming there was a call."

"Well, of course there was a call."

"That's what I think, too."

"Is my husband expected to recognise a voice he has only heard once?"

"Might help him if he could. I believe his yarn, but thousands wouldn't, and there's still quite a number of chaps going about thinking he might be the one to give me my quietus that evening. I'd expect you to be glad he had a chance to clear himself."

She gobbled like a gobbledegook, but she raised no further objections.

"Suppose I don't recognise any of them?" Gordon asked unhappily.

"That'll be just too bad; we shall have to think of something else. But let's cross that bridge when we come to it." He moved expectantly towards a door, any door, it didn't matter, so long as he got his message through, that time was passing and they might as well get a wiggle on.

" Give the lady a chance to get on at her end," he advised, " then we'll get cracking."

" What on earth am I to say ? "

" Good heavens, man, you're a husband, aren't you ? That usually polishes up a chap's imagination. Say you're a salesman, be a crank who's pestered by obscene callers on the line, be the police, if you like, most people don't realise rozzers like to do their jobs in person and have to have a second officer sitting in before they can take a statement, say your garden's been ruined by the other fellow's dog, no, I know you haven't got a garden, and probably he hasn't got a dog, but while he's explaining that'll be your chance to discover if you've heard the voice before. And if the wrong person answers, hang on till you get the right one."

Gordon did better than Crook had anticipated, rattling off his various stories, varying his tone of voice, and once, when he was rung off impatiently, dialling the number again.

" Fly," thought Crook. " Well, I suppose he'd need to be to stand up to that human icicle." But it did occur to him that the visit to the Fiddlers' Rest mightn't be the only indiscretion of which the chap could be convicted. Still, no skin off his nose. Let him get the info. he wanted, and you wouldn't see him for dust.

They got all their connections but one. Crook looked dissatisfied. " Some other chap up de-worming the lawn, well, why not ? Can't expect to have the whole show to myself. We'll have to try again later."

" If you say so, but it's not necessary."

" Meaning you've recognised the voice ? You're dead sure ? You'll have to give this evidence in court."

" That'll be all right." There was a kind of vindictive confidence about the man that supported his claim. " Want me to come along ? "

It was Crook's turn to gape. "Come along where?"

"Aren't you going to the station?"

"Without as much proof as 'ud fill a thimble? The police ain't brought up on fairy-tales, any they know they make up themselves. They'd simply say we'd put our heads together and X has only to deny our story—no, it isn't us that's going to clap him under covers, he's got to sign his own death warrant. Now, don't leave your office to-night till Bill turns up. That's Bill Parsons, my A.D.C. Look out of the window and you'll likely see him waiting by the Superb. Take a good look, so's you'll know him again."

"There's no need for him to come," said Gordon uneasily. "I'm perfectly capable of keeping an appointment under my own steam."

"You don't understand," said Crook. "You recognised X. Suppose X recognised you? I've taken chances enough in this case. I've wasted several days in hospital and I've lost a perfectly good hat. I'm playing for safety from now on. And you'll be all right with Bill. Couldn't be safer with the Lord Chief Justice. By the way, which one did you pick?"

Alistair told him.

"So we do agree about something. Now, just before we part, add your office phone number to this list, just in case, and it 'ud help us all if you could forget about mentioning the wallet to the police till, say, after 6 p.m. I'm always easier in my mind when they ain't sitting in."

From the window Alistair watched the spherical brown figure skip jauntily into the Superb. A tall dark chap with a face you wouldn't forget easily, got into the passenger seat.

"So that's Bill," reflected Alistair. Coming through the hall he collected the wallet and put it in his pocket. Now that Crook had gone his elation was fading; the only satisfaction he could find was in assuring Fiona he might be late for dinner, no, he couldn't give her any details, it was a closed shop affair, and why didn't she ask one of her buddies in or—better still—go out herself?

:: ::

" Times I'm sorry for donkeys," Crook was observing to Bill Parsons, " the way they have to go here, there and everywhere lugging other fellows' burdens, but you have to admit they set us a good example. Stick their solid little hoofs down and nothing short of the Atom Bomb 'ull move 'em. Now I'll check up on this lot and you tackle the Somerset House end. If we don't meet anywhere along the road, collect Gordon and bring him along to the Duck and Daisy round about 5 p.m. Seems a nice poetical idea to finish the job where it began." And for an instant he was back in that lugubrious bar, with the fog outside reflected by the gloomy faces within, until the whole place was suddenly lighted up by Torquil Holland and his gang. " I'll see if Jim can let us have a bit of privacy, he won't want trouble in his bar, and he's got no Mrs. Jim to object to the loan of a room, it could be a long session."

He went bumbling round, interviewing people who received him with surprise, suspicion or indignation as the case might be, and he was safely back in 123 Bloomsbury Street when Bill returned from Somerset House with the information that was going to put the lid on the case.

" Curtain rises, last act," he observed, looking affectionately round his office with its drab brown walls and stacks of papers, as if secretly he wondered when he'd be seeing them again.

" Remember the last scene in Hamlet, Bill ? Corpses all over the place. Well, the heads are going to roll to-night and let's hope mine ain't one of them."

CHAPTER XIV

AT FIVE O'CLOCK Crook was ringing the side bell at the Duck and Daisy. Jim Prentiss, who had been warned to expect him, opened the door in person. He expressed surprise that Crook had come alone.

" I gathered from the message there was going to be a—well, a kind of gathering," he acknowledged.

" That's what it will be. I wanted a word with you first, though."

" You'll take something to drink, Mr. Crook? In the private part of the house licensing hours don't apply."

" You do yourself very well," Crook told him, and indeed it was surprising to find a room freshly-papered and painted and a good quality carpet laid down when you remembered the general rather scruffy effect of the bar.

" It's my hobby," said Jim in a voice of a man who doesn't wish to seem to boast. " I'm going to do some of the other rooms now. My predecessor can't have spent five pounds on paper and paint all the time he was here."

" Not afraid you'll find yourself calling the banns?" murmured Crook, but Jim said: " It 'ud be a bit late for that. And somehow I don't fancy the idea, not at my time of life."

" And who's the pot to call the kettle black?" Crook agreed. " Jim, there's something I want you to do, if you can. That voice you heard over the phone saying I wasn't coming along that night—do you think there's a chance you'd recognise it again, if you were to hear it?"

Jim looked flabbergasted. " Oh come, Mr. Crook, a voice I never heard before?"

" That's the point. Are you dead certain you'd never heard it before?"

" It didn't ring a bell."

" Because you weren't expecting a bell to ring. But—well, you couldn't swear it was mine ? "

" I didn't really think about it. I said it might have been a message, but you know how it is that time of the evening. It didn't occur to me it mightn't be genuine. For one thing, who'd know you were expected ? "

" The lot that was expecting me ? "

Jim turned sharply. " You mean, you think it was one of them ? "

" You said yourself there couldn't be many people who knew. There was Gordon's message as well—don't forget that. By the way, he'll be here this evening."

Jim stiffened slowly. " Mr. Crook, I have to say I don't like this, I don't like it a bit. Are you going to ask me to say his was the voice ? "

" I'm not going to ask you to say anything you aren't prepared to swear to in court. But—get this—I'm not really concerned with anyone's feelings but my client's. The rest can go jump in the lake for me, and for their own sakes I hope they can swim. All I'm asking you is to speak up if you do recognise the voice, and if not for ever hold your peace. Now, while we're waiting for the party to arrive—there's six Brigadiers, Bill, Gordon, you and me . . ."

" I'll have to be in the bar when it opens, Mr. Crook.'

" How about your girl, Sally, that's as smart as a whip ? Don't tell me you're never off the premises during opening hours because I shouldn't believe you. Anyway, we could get the drinks mixed, looks more hospitable. . . ."

It passed through Jim's mind that Crook didn't look unlike a fairy-tale ogre preparing to have a feast of human flesh. He had produced a slip of paper and said, " I thought beer for the young chaps, and a Scotch for the doctor—better make it a double, ditto for Gordon—I don't know how well he holds his drink but this could be quite an occasion for him—then there's Bill . . ."

" Just a minute, Mr. Crook. I'll make a note. Of course I could bring the bottles along."

But Crook said he hadn't got all night and it wasn't exactly a social occasion.

When Jim had made a record and gone to prepare the glasses Crook wandered round the room, stopping in front of a print of Sir Alfred Munnings's " Derby Day "—not that he was a betting man himself, a nice little mare called Murder saw him through—then the side bell rang again and Crook sang out, " I'll let 'em in " and there were Bill and Gordon, the latter rigid as a ladder, Bill looking as though he'd been born playing poker and wouldn't know now how to wear any other kind of face.

Gordon said awkwardly, " Nice room," and Crook said: " Wonder if it's ever used. Like a Victorian parlour . . ." and then Jim came back with the tray; of his own accord he'd added a dish of potato crisps and some nuts and olives.

" Very festive," said Crook. Probably you couldn't have found four less festive-looking men in the whole of the U.K.

The Brigadiers came in a body, chattering all the way from the corner.

" Does Crook really suppose he's going to clap his hands and yell 'Hey Presto!' and Walter Smith is going to materialise out of thin air ? " reflected Evelyn.

Rupert sounded surly. " Someone ought to tell him this masked ball solution is fearfully *vieux jeu*."

" Oh, don't do him out of his bit of limelight," pleaded Colin, charitably. " It can't be all jam even for him. And if he enjoys being ringmaster, making the elephants sit up and beg and putting the seals through their balancing act . . ."

" God give me strength ! " exploded Jos Wymark. " For His sake try and use the brains with which He has seen fit to endow you. Haven't you realised yet that Crook's strength lies in the fact that he doesn't give a tinker's curse for any one of us as individuals, he's the man on the job ? Oh, I dare say he plays up very skilfully, I'm always expecting to see him chuck one of the girls under the chin, but don't let that deceive you. He'd see the lot of us strung up, Jim included, if that was the only way he could get Torquil out of clink. And do you notice he always talks of him as 'my client'? If any of you have got anything to hide you'd do better to drop dead now."

His violence, as unexpected as it seemed uncharacteristic, rocked them all back on their heels. Their voices died suddenly, and they came into the Duck and Daisy close together, like a pack of hounds, stiff with suspicion. Crook moved forward and made the introductions. When he mentioned Gordon's name both the girls drew back.

"What's he doing here?" Julie inquired harshly.

"He's going to try and help us to find an alternative name for Walter Smith. I thought that's what we were all out for."

"Still on that lay," said Rupert. "Do you still think he's one of us?"

"It's a bit late in the day to introduce anyone new," Crook protested. "This case has been going on and on like the dormouse's tail. It's about time we tied a bow on the end of it. Things are complicated enough. But, for your satisfaction, I don't mind telling you you and your two chums are out of it. I mean, you couldn't have had a hand in putting out Paul's light, because I've been checking and counter-checking most of the day, and the old nanny-goat in the flat under yours (his obstinate chin indicated the courteous, attentive figure of Evelyn) will go to town on the fact of the three of you playing rock and roll till after midnight."

"Not rock and roll," Evelyn protested.

"Let's not get bogged down over a phrase." Crook said it quite pleasantly but Evelyn felt a *frisson* down his spine. It was the first time Crook had seemed completely ruthless, and he realised that of them all only Dr. Wymark had got the chap sized up. "She's got a pretty nice line in words herself. 'If I'd wanted to live in a zoo, Mr. Crook,' she said, 'I'd have got myself born a chimpanzee.'"

Rupert, who was also feeling the strain of the occasion, said impudently, "And she didn't? I hadn't noticed."

But it fell absolutely flat, not a glimmer of a smile. Gordon was looking fixedly at the tray of drinks, but so far as the rest of the party was concerned they could have been the original cups of cold pizen. Indeed, no one else seemed to realise they were there, and he wasn't too sure of his own control—shocking if the glass tilted and spilt—so he said nothing either.

Bill looked impervious, Jim was clearly more ill-at-ease with every second that passed—but then he had his licence to think of, and, like the police, he wouldn't put anything past his eccentric customer.

" That was three of you out," Crook continued. " That left me with the doctor and the two girls."

" It can't have been Jos," protested Colin. " He was in the Midlands."

" Northampton. It ain't the North Pole. And Paul wasn't knocked on the head till 11 p.m. I know about the fog but the trains weren't above an hour and a half late on that line. . . ."

" But Jos wouldn't know about the showdown in the bar here," Ruth said. " None of us anticipated it."

" No," Julie agreed. " He hadn't seen Torquil that night or Paul either."

" You don't have to see chaps face to face to get *au fait* with a situation," Crook pointed out in patient tones. ' There's that telephone call Paul had at the Casbah. You all seem to have taken for granted that it was him making it, but he could have been receiving it, couldn't he ? "

There was an instant's silence ; then Rupert admitted, " Yes, I suppose he could."

" We're pretty sure that's when the rendezvous in the passage was fixed, and we don't know that he didn't himself give the wig-wag to the chap who was going to douse his light half an hour or so later. Mind you, I'm not makin' accusations. I'm just clearin' the ground."

" Oh, we appreciate that, Mr. Crook," said Jos in a hard voice. " And have I got an alibi for 11 p.m. ? Answer—no. But then I didn't expect to need one. I got a meal on the way back, and I doubt if anyone would remember me there, I didn't throw the soup at the mirror or spill the salt, nothing to attract attention."

" No sudden calls after your return ? " murmured Crook. " I mean, you do contrive to find yourself in the most unexpected places, don't you ? I seem to remember us meeting on a couple of occasions recently, unexpected by me, anyway."

Ruth, sitting with her chin on her folded fist, said abruptly, " Jos is a doctor, Mr. Crook. Had you forgotten ? "

" So was Palmer. So was Smethurst. You should make a list some time. Still, I haven't accused anyone yet."

" Aren't Julie and I lucky—that we can alibi each other, I mean ? I rang her up just after eleven, about the time someone was attacking Paul, and she was washing her hair."

" She told you so ? "

" The landlady did."

" What the soldier said ain't evidence. I mean, say she was on the stand, she couldn't actually prove Sweetie-pie was in the bathroom, could she ? "

Julie spoke for the first time ; she'd been regarding Gordon with the sort of loathing a fanatical Christian of olden time might have bestowed on the heathen Chinese. " I told her when I came in I was going to wash my hair."

" And she offered to lend a hand ? "

" Of course not. We're all independent these days, we can even wash our own hair without help."

" See what I mean ? I could tell you I was going to bed with a stomach-ache, but unless someone actually sees me under the blankets, which heaven forbid, there's no proof I didn't spend the night in Piccadilly Circus."

" She would see the light was on. There's a transom above the door," Juliet insisted.

" All that proves is that the light's on. It don't prove there's anyone in the room."

" The door was locked. That could be proved because someone tried to get in."

" And you yelled out that you were washing your hair and happened to mention your name."

" Of course I didn't. You can't carry on a conversation with your head in a basin. I heard the handle turn."

"Well, yes, that's your story and I'm not saying it's not true, but all it proves is that the door was locked, and doors can be locked from the outside as well as the in. Now tell me this. Why didn't you ring your buddy back when you emerged from the taps? I mean, it could have been something urgent."

"My buddy? Oh, you mean Ruth. Well, I didn't know she'd telephoned."

"Meaning Mrs. Whosit didn't pass the message on?"

"I didn't ask her to pass it on," explained Ruth. "She's as deaf as a post, I didn't think she'd ever get a number over the air. I rang up Julie next morning."

"At all events it gives Ruth an alibi," urged Colin. "She couldn't have been telephoning from Maida Vale soon after eleven if she'd been meeting Paul in Brandon Passage."

"Not if she can prove she was ringing from her own flat," Crook admitted. "Anyone see you come in?" he added, to Ruth.

The girl looked startled. "No. Not that I can recall, and at this stage no one would be likely to remember, even if they had."

"See why I said I still had three possibles, two of whom say they saw Paul that evening. Now we come to last night. . . ."

"We were all glued to our telephones then," Rupert protested. "That is, I was—Good heavens, have we got to prove that? We can't even alibi each other, because you saw to it we should all be at different addresses."

"You telephoned me, Mr. Crook," Colin reminded him.

"The time I had in mind was round about 10.30. I know one Brigadier who wasn't at home, and that was Dr. Jos Wymark."

"Well, but Ruth's already pointed out that Jos is a doctor, you can't expect to be able to tie him down."

"As Mr. Crook well knows, I was called out to a patient and on the way back I ran into a street accident. For your information, the victim died in hospital this morning. I shall have to attend the inquest."

" He was very hospitable," Crook went on, as though the doctor hadn't spoken. " Insisted on getting me a drink. . ."

" Which Jim gave us on the house," Jos capped him.

" I hope, Mr. Crook, you're not suggesting there was something wrong with the beer."

" Not with the beer, but what went into it. Ever heard of a Mickey Finn ? "

" It's some kind of dope, isn't it ? " inquired Rupert.

" Are you suggesting you had drugged beer in my public-house ? " Jim looked as if he might explode.

" I darn well know I did. Though I didn't realise it till I was on my way home. And, believe it or not, I caught sight of my old buddy, Dr. Wymark, lurking in the Casbah, oh, don't misunderstand me. He just wanted to make sure I got back all right. Called a taxi for me and everything. Didn't you, Doctor ? "

" I told you I liked to play Watson to your Holmes."

" Enough to make Holmes turn in his grave finding himself made a monkey of. I don't mind telling you now that I was scared out of my wits when I heard those footsteps coming up behind me, and there's not many can boast they've made Arthur Crook quake in his natty Number Ten Oxfords. When that load of misery at your flea-pit "—he nodded towards Ruth—" wouldn't let me in because it was after hours—no admission for the last twenty minutes of the programme, which stops at 10.45—I thought I was a goner."

" Are you telling us that Jos knew about the dope ? " Rupert's voice was incredulous.

" Oh, yes," said Crook softly. " He knew all right."

" But you're here all in one piece. What happened ? "

" My Guardian Angel had to pull something out of the sack, and it had to be fast and it had to be good. I must have passed out in the taxi," he added. " How the heck did you get me up the stairs of No. 2 ? I blacked out like a Christy Minstrel."

" It wouldn't be the first time I've toted a near-corpse up a staircase," Jos told him. " Anyway, you were in a lot better shape by the time I took you home."

" I go koko," cried Colin. " I mean, I don't know where

we are. A minute ago you were accusing Jos of doping your beer."

"You can't have been listening," Crook reproved him. "I said I had a drink at the pub and it had been doped. That's all."

"But—you can't mean *Jim* doped it. But why? Oh, no. *He's* not Walter Smith."

And Colin added simply, "You're bonkers, Mr. Crook. How on earth does Jim come into this?"

"Of course he's not bonkers," shouted Gordon, unable to restrain himself any longer. "I'm sorry, Mr. Crook, but I've had enough. I recognised his voice on the phone before I knew who he was, and I recognised it again to-night as soon as I heard it. That's the one that spoke to me over the telephone and told me my appointment with you was cancelled." In his excitement he sprang to his feet, pointing to Jim like an excited schoolboy. "I spoke to you all this morning, but I never had any doubt. . . ."

"Are you, by the way, being troubled by obscene callers?" added Crook.

"Was that you? Fancy that! Well, Mr. Crook, it's a nice little plot, but you know better than me you couldn't take that story into court. You tell a chap to ring up So-and-So and get him to say, 'Yes, that's the one I spoke to before.'"

"He didn't know who he was speaking to," Crook assured him. "I just gave him the numbers. He didn't know when he came here to-night, it could have been any of them."

"But Jim had a message himself," protested Colin.

"Who says so?"

"He told us."

"See what I mean about proof? He told you he'd had a message. He said it came through about seven. At seven two things happened. I was bopped over the head and Sweetie-pie here"—he indicated Julie—"came into the bar for a snack. Funny he didn't give her the message, wouldn't you say? Or maybe not so odd when you come to think of it."

" Are you saying he never had a message ? "

" No one's come forward who admits to sending it."

" But how did he know you were expected that evening, Mr. Crook ? You only told me and Julie that afternoon, and we only told the others. None of us told Jim."

Crook sighed. " Proof again. The utmost you can say is that you didn't tell Jim."

" Who would tell him ? "

" I don't think his niece would leave him in the dark."

There is a childhood's game that ends with " All Fall Down." No one actually fell, but the impression of a lot of stupefied bodies lying around was achieved.

" He told me that first evening—my sister's girl goes around with this crowd, and I've got so used to adding two and two and making it ninety-six I overlooked the fact that now and again they actually do make four."

Rupert turned and met Julie's eye ; it was clear and inexpressive as ice.

" I don't believe it," stammered Colin. " Julie's been Torquil's man from the beginning."

" Criminals are never anyone's man but their own. Well, look how his buddies ganged up against Paul (Aslett, in fact, Walter Smith's pardner) the minute he looked like being dangerous. Mind you, I don't blame them. Self-preservation's the first law, and he'd have sold them up the creek as readily as they sold him. But did it never strike any of you as a bit convenient that he should surface in Jim's bar, and get himself transferred instanter ? Oh, no, it was all very neatly fixed, and you all fell for it."

" You've said a lot about proof to-night, Mr. Crook," Jim observed smoothly. " I take it you've got proof of what you've just said."

" Tell 'em, Bill," said Crook.

Bill took two pieces of paper from his pocket. " True copies of entries in the records of Somerset House," he told them. " Number One is a marriage certificate between Alice Prentiss and one William Danesfoot, in 1938. The other records the birth of a daughter, subsequently christened Ruth."

Ruth had her hands deep in the pockets of her jersey coat. "All right, Jim's my uncle," she acknowledged. "There's no crime in that. . ."

"You never told us," cried Colin.

"That was my wish," Jim assured them. "I've always made it a rule as a licensee not to give drinks on credit. I've seen what it leads to. You allow chaps to chalk up the last couple, then when you want to collect you find they've melted into some other manor, and you're left holding the baby. But you can see for yourselves how awkward it could be for me to refuse my niece's friends. And anyway, they can say what they like about democracy, but don't tell me it would do my niece any good to have it known her uncle was a publican."

"Have half London trying to chalk up drinks," Crook agreed.

"Ruth has an important job in this laboratory of hers. I'm very proud of her, so are her parents. There's your explanation."

"Fair enough," Crook agreed. "Mind you, I think it's all poppycock, but it's possible you felt that way. But there's something else I'd like to hear her explain." He turned to Ruth. "Why did you tell us you'd seen my client going into the Casbah that night, wearing his raincoat?"

"You'd impressed on us the necessity for not keeping anything back, no matter how damaging."

"Ah, but damaging to whom? That's the point. If you hadn't given that evidence—and you didn't tell that yarn until I took over the case, you didn't mention it to the police—they wouldn't have assumed the bloodstained coat they found in the train was his that was missing."

Rupert suddenly stood up. "Penny's dropped at last, Mr. Crook. You mean, Ruth couldn't have seen him wearing that coat, because at the time Torquil reached the Casbah she was in the news cinema."

"I wondered which of you would get there first," Crook told him. "Funny thing, if I hadn't tried to get in myself last night, escaping from my guardian angel, and there's nothing truer than that they come in the most unexpected guise—I wouldn't have known they didn't admit the public after 10.25." He turned to Ruth. "We know you were there, because you left your scarf to provide yourself with an alibi, but we also know that Torquil didn't reach the Casbah till Heinz had left it, and he noticed the clock next door and that said 10.30. Young Holland never saw Heinz, I asked him particularly, so you see . . ."

"Any proof that he didn't see him? Beyond his word, I mean?" inquired Jim silkily.

Crook just stared; he looked as if his eyes were going to fall out.

"Proof!" he exclaimed. "What are you talking about? Chap's my client. No, she didn't need to go to the Casbah. Uncle Jim made the arrangement—remember she had a little confab with him before she marched out, under cover of buying everyone drinks, and at 11 p.m. she went along to the passage . . ."

"Why should you suppose she went there?" demanded Jos. "It could be Jim."

"I had a trunk call that evening as soon as the bar closed," said Jim. "And that's something that can be proved."

"She had to get the brief-case with the loot in it," Crook said. "It was all very neat when you come to think of it. They'd been carrying on this system of exchange under all your noses. That was the reason for the practically identical brief-cases. Paul would put his down and collect hers, while she delivered the goods to the boss here. And that's what she did that night. Only she couldn't leave her case, because it might be recognised. So she slipped along to the Duck and Daisy, rang Julie from here. . . ."

"And of course she didn't leave a message. Say Sugar had bound her flowing locks with a towel and run down to the phone, she was going to think it queer no one answered when she dialled the flat in Maida Vale. And no one would, because there wasn't anyone there."

"In a minute," said Ruth, "you're going to explain how I could walk through the streets in a coat dripping with blood —Mr. Gordon was noticed at once. . . ."

" You were wearing a scarlet mac," Crook reminded her. " Plastic, which they tell me washes like a dream, no need to send it to a cleaner—not wearing it to-night, I notice."

" It tore," said Ruth indifferently. " These plastic macs do. I've taken a leaf out of Julie's book and bought a nylon one."

" And the old one's somewhere in a rubbish tip."

" I suppose so. You've forgotten one thing, though. How did I break the electric light bulb ? Climb on Paul's shoulders ? "

" You had a nice long red brolly, just the job."

" It was a fog that night, not a thunderstorm. You don't need an umbrella in a fog."

" B-but you did have it, Ruth," stammered Colin. " You said you always brought it to meetings to wake people up or something. You said you'd laddered a woman's stocking."

" And when we got to the top of Marston Street last evening there was a car drawn up by the kerb, with a lady in the driving-seat. I was trying to hail it when it drove off all of a sudden."

" Do you mean that was waiting for *you* ? " whispered Julie.

" If you're on the verge of passin' out and a lady you've met before suddenly appears in a car and says, ' Hop in, Mr. Crook, let me drive you home,' what do you do ? ' Thanks a million, lady,' and in you get. No witnesses, and when they find the body in a gutter in an alley it's Old Man Crook had one over the eight once too often, taken a tumble or fallen under the wheels of a car, too bad it didn't stop, but we're all in such a hurry these days, and when it's a matter of the oldsters, well, there's plenty more where they come from. I suppose you'd vanished from the bar—not a peep out of you, Walter, when I left—to get the young lady on the blower and tell her to come round and collect the wallet—well, you knew things were winding up and you wouldn't want to be found with that in your possession—so drop it through the old man's letter-box, and let him do the explaining. Only, of course, he ain't going to be in any situation for that. What they didn't allow for was Dr. Jos obeyin' his hunch, and by that time it was too late to get the wallet back. It's a wonder to me," he added, " they didn't try and plug the doctor, too."

A voice none of them recognised as Julie's said, " I should like to kill you myself. To do that to Torquil . . ." Not, Crook noted, to Arthur Crook.

" No jumping the gun," exclaimed Crook sharply, and then Jim said : " This is where I telephone to the police, Mr. Crook, and while we're waiting for them you better think of a more convincing explanation of how you got the wallet back."

" You do that," Crook agreed cordially. " And I don't think I have to worry about the wallet. You see, it's like I said, criminals always slip up sooner or later. There's a general belief that if you disguise your hand-writing it can't be identified. That ain't so. An expert, who's got a specimen of your natural hand, can generally equate the two. And in any case not many criminals remember to disguise their figuring. Now, there's the figure ' 2 ' in my address. Right ? "

They nodded like a lot of mandarins.

" And I got all of you to write down your phone numbers last night."

" But you didn't ask Jim—did you ? "

" Well, no, that might have seemed a bit remarkable. But I did get him to write down details of the drinks I ordered this evening and that, come to think of it, no one's tasted. And there's a couple of 2's here, and my friend, Bill, knows a chap . . ."

Jim laughed harshly. " Criminals aren't the only ones that make mistakes, Mr. Crook. If there's any address on that envelope, you put it there yourself, and if you think you can make anything of that . . ."

Crook smote himself on the forehead. " You know what they say—old men forget. Of course there wasn't any address. I remember now. A nice blank envelope—though it 'ud register a nice fingerprint—only, seeing you never set eyes on the wallet, how come you could be so sure ? "

There was a scream from Gordon and he ducked down beside his chair.

" Mr. Crook, take care, he's armed."

At the same instant there was a sort of groan as Evelyn toppled to the carpet.

" I told you it was going to be bodies, bodies everywhere," muttered Crook. The thought flashed like lightning through his mind that women don't know how to spend money even when they have it. Surely Fiona could have found an investment that would pay a better dividend than the cowering Alistair. Then the thought rushed on into the dark and he forgot Gordon altogether.

Jim Prentiss had backed up against a little sideboard and —shades of the flea-pit, thought Crook, he had a little snub-nosed pistol in his hand. Must have been prepared for any emergency, Crook supposed. And a nasty shock when the lawyer turned up brisk and chipper and sassy, as the American poet put it. Outside the room life seemed to roll on as usual. Glasses clinked in the bar, someone dropped four coppers into the public phone box in the passage. Prentiss said, " That'll be enough. Next person that moves or tries to make trouble or I'll use this. And don't think I'm bluffing." He swung the weapon in Julie's direction. " The girl gets it first," he said. They couldn't, reflected Crook, have done it better on the telly.

In the room the silence held till suddenly Ruth shouted, " Uncle Jim, look out ! "

Jim looked down, seemed to stumble and went crashing to the ground with Bill on top of him ; the pistol in his hand went off with a noise that seemed to raise the roof. It clattered to the carpet and Bill kicked it into a corner. In the ensuing melée someone trod on Evelyn's hand and he yelled, " D'you mind, I've only got two."

" Shouldn't be on the carpet anyway," muttered Rupert, and Crook said, " There's gratitude for you. Who d'you think pulled the enemy down ? A very nice job," he added, hauling the young man to his feet. " That faint even took me in for a minute, though I suppose the doc wasn't deceived even that long."

"A trick?" Colin grinned faintly, relief as much as anything, goodness knew there wasn't much to grin about. "Didn't think you had it in you. I suppose Ruth . . ."

"Don't say a word," barked Jim, and Jos said in a voice like a granite slab: "She won't. It all plays your way in the end, doesn't it? Now you can tell any yarn you like, and there's no one to turn Queen's Evidence. Not that she'd have done that anyway."

He was on his knees beside the chair where Ruth lay back, but he rose as he spoke. Gordon also came shakily to his feet.

"You mean she . . . but this is awful. Get a doctor, get a doctor."

"Get two," amended Crook brutally. "Then we can have this lunatic certified."

"I'm a doctor," Jos told the frantic man. "And the whole of Harley Street couldn't help her now. There aren't very many instantaneous poisons available, even to a girl who works in a lab but she's got one of them. It was over before you'd got her partner on his feet."

"So that was why?" said Colin. "I thought she was trying to warn him."

"I've told you, people like that don't think of anyone but themselves. She knew she hadn't a chance. Oh yes, she put paid to your previous pal, and Uncle Jim will be the first to say so when they get him in the box. And you don't need to look so startled. You want to brush up your criminal history a bit. It's no wonder the ancient warriors feared the Amazons more than anything in trousers. Ah, here they come!"

There was a commotion in the passage outside, the door burst open and the policemen whom the resourceful Sally had summoned at the sound of that first scream, shouldered their way into the room.

"What's going on, Mr. Crook?" one of them said.

"O.K.," said Crook. "You take over. And when you've

got a minute to spare it might occur to you to wonder why a chap who hasn't bothered to put a lick of paint anywhere for more than two years, should suddenly buckle down and start redecorating a room that from the look of it no one ever uses, except for telephoning. Well, use your eyes. No comfy chair, no telly, no radio, no books or papers scattered around—I wouldn't mind betting there's nothing in the sideboard."

"What's happened to the young lady?" asked one of the policemen and Jos replied in a voice that shocked them all: "She's dead. Even your lot won't be able to get a statement from her."

"Have it your own way," said Crook resignedly, "but if you should still be interested in the Hunter jewels it might pay you to take a look under that nice print of 'Derby Day'. I was pottering round while mine host got the drinks and my guess is there's a hollow space there, cupboard maybe with the door removed and a panel fitted. Well, why not? The stuff 'ud be too hot to handle for another couple of years. And by then he'd be ready to move on. Oh, it's not a new idea. Think of Christie with his bodies behind the wallpaper. . . ."

Jos spoke suddenly, cutting Crook off in midstream. He spoke across the room to Jim Prentiss.

"If you were thinking of trying to saddle Ruth with the attack on Crook," he said, "you'll be wasting your time. Ruth was out with me that evening, and I'll swear to it till Kingdom Come."

CHAPTER XV

WHEN LADY CONSTANCE was told that her jewellery had been recovered she gave a little start, said hurriedly, "Well, that's good news, isn't it?" and later confided to her husband: "Well, it is good news, of course, but disappointing in a way. I really had looked forward to getting something new . . ."

When she heard about Ruth she forgot about the jewellery and said, "Poor girl! She must have been led astray."

It was the kindest epitaph Ruth was to know.

: : : :

The authorities were unable to establish a case against Jim Prentiss for the murder of Aslett. He protested from start to finish that it had been no part of any pre-arranged plan. Ruth had been deputed to meet him and collect the brief-case. According to the story, as retailed by the sole survivor of the trio, the man had turned nasty, uttered threats and Ruth had slashed out at him with a convenient brick. "She didn't know he was dead when she left him," Jim insisted. "It was as much of a shock to her as to me."

Well, there it was, and you could believe as much or as little as you liked. There was no one to give contrary evidence; Crook was convinced that Prentiss would have blamed the attack in Bloomsbury Street on the girl, if possible, but the doctor stuck to his testimony. Even without a murder charge they had plenty on Prentiss, whom they were able to identify with the chap who'd carried off the body of the pseudo-Jack Aslett three years before. He'd had to sign documents, and though he hadn't used his own name the handwriting experts had him trapped. They found bank accounts in three names, too.

"Not that they'll ever be able to pin Luzky's murder on to him or any member of the gang," Crook acknowledged. "For one thing, there's no actual proof it was murder at all.

He was a boozer and he could have slipped on the towpath on a wet day; he could have put himself in, heaven knows he hadn't much to live for, he could even have been knocked off by one of his own nationals, but for myself I think Jim or Aslett did it. Why contact him unless he was going to be some use to them, and he wasn't so much use so long as he was alive? But here was a chap no one was going to miss, specially if someone took over his identity. Maybe in a sober moment he learnt too much, blackmail's always dangerous to the amateur."

He made these observations to Torquil Holland, who had been graciously released with a free pardon for a crime he hadn't committed. His evidence would be required at the trial, so he'd had to scrub the expedition, but since the world's full of lost causes he wasn't unemployed long.

"What still foxes me," he acknowledged, "is why the gang picked on the Peace Brigade for a cover. We're such small beer. . . ."

"Well, he wasn't much more than a midget himself," said Crook dryly. "And I dare say they wanted a nice umbrella to scramble under, and what better than a body that's trying to do a bit of good? That and Jim getting the pub. A pub's always good cover, gives a chap an air of such respectability. He was a genuine publican, you know, had a couple before this, same story each time, sticks about three years and then moves out. And, why not? He's a free agent, no hostages to fortune. It's a funny thing," he added, going off at a bit of a tangent, "that girl's parents, his sister and her husband, are decent hard-working tradesfolk, objecting to their daughter's association with what they regard as a Red organisation. Poor devils, I'm glad I didn't have to be the one to tell them. There's times I'm sorry for the police, really I am."

"The one I'm sorry for is Jos. He was pretty badly smitten."

"And the poet who said we needs must love the highest when we see it forgot there's another side to the medal. Don't quote me, but I shall always believe he could have stopped her taking that tablet, only why should he? He told me he had his first suspicion the night before when we came out of Marston Street and he recognised her car. He was just going to hail her when she drove off, and when he rang the next morning she swore she hadn't left the house the whole evening."

"I suppose he could have been wrong." But Crook shook his head. "Not chaps like that. No, he took the knock all right."

"I hear he's going to work in the industrial north now this trouble's over," said Torquil. Already he seemed to have shaken off the marks of his prison experience. "And Rupert's father's sending him overseas on the firm's behalf, and Colin's murmuring something about getting married. Fact is, we're falling apart at the seams."

But he didn't sound troubled. Chaps who live in the middle of next week never are. There's always a fresh cause over the hill—he made Crook think of young Avery Greatorex, another zealot who'd spent his life like water and now lay in a grave in a strange land, fighting for a pipe-dream. It was odd that after so many years Crook still remembered him.

Steps came up the stairs, the door opened, Julie came in.

"What on earth are you doing here ?" Torquil exclaimed.

"I trailed you, you ape. Besides, I wanted to see Mr. Crook. I thought perhaps we could all have a final drink before I set out."

"Set out where ?" Torquil inquired.

"I've got a job, a good one, lead in a number one touring company. Probably go half-round the world before we're through. We might even meet in the middle." She gave Torquil a blue shimmering glance that would have blinded most men. Even Crook felt himself blink.

"You'll have to stay for the trial," Torquil protested.

"No, why ? I haven't got any evidence. I'm as free as a bird."

"Birds get caught in cages," Crook assured her.

"Perhaps some of them like cages. How about that drink ?"

Torquil looked at his watch. "I'll join you in, say,

twenty minutes. I've got to ring a chap." At the door he turned. "Where'll I find you?"

"The Bosun's Whistle. Emery Street." Torquil vanished. "It'll always be like that, sugar," said Crook gently. "You might as well set your heart on an air bubble."

"Tell me something, Mr. Crook. When things were going wrong, in this last case, say, did you ever think you might throw it up?"

Crook puffed like the Æsopian frog. "Don't say things like that to me, sugar. I might have an apoplectic fit. The day I throw up a case they can cart me along to the Eventide Home."

"Well, there you are!" said Juliet, with every appearance of logic.

"O.K. If that's the way it is he might as well give up the ghost now. One of these days he'll come toiling up Everest and find you waiting for him on the summit."

"You know such a lot," said Juliet gently, "you ought to be able to give me a hint or two. It isn't that I jib at climbing Everest, but I'd sooner climb it in company."

"There's always the tortoise and the hare," the little lawyer reminded her. "Anybody's money would have been on the hare. And don't remind me the tortoise won by cheating. When we get to Heaven we'll all play fair, but so long as we're mortal we have to use the weapons that come to hand. But even so," he would up, as she spun out of the door, "you'd be safer to stick to the stage."

: : : :

Down on the borders of Epping Forest an old chap called George Leavis lighted an illegal fire and began plucking a pair of pigeons he'd brought down a bit earlier in the day. Born of gipsy parents, he could light a fire in any weather and cook without a pan. He must have been one of the last free men left in England. Rates, taxes, licences, these meant nothing to him, and he hadn't bought an insurance stamp in twenty years. From the capacious pockets of his coat he produced a bottle of milk he'd filched from a door-step, a loaf he'd transferred in a flash from an unattended baker's van, some eggs he'd coaxed silently from under a hen who was, praise the pigs, laying wild. There was a sharpish wind and he pulled the coat closer round his shoulders. It had been a bit of luck finding that left in a telephone booth on his last visit to London. He'd popped inside to press Button B just in case, and there it was lying on the floor. One of the buttons didn't match, but what was that to him?

There hadn't been a soul in sight when he peered out of the box, and chaps that can afford to leave a good coat lying about in such weather can't need it much. But anyway, if there had been any hue and cry after it later on, how was he to know, a dotty old tramp who'd had no education, never listened to the wireless and couldn't even read?

www.ingramcontent.com/pod-product-compliance
Ingram Content Group UK Ltd.
Pitfield, Milton Keynes, MK11 3LW, UK
UKHW022312280225
455674UK00004B/280

9 781471 910227